Ballards Crossing

Falsely accused of murdering two friends, Mark Dalton had no choice but to take to the fugitive trail. Now he has a $5,000 price on his head, wanted dead or alive.

Three men were responsible for framing Mark: Randers, the real killer, and his two associates, Tollard and Cordray. The gang now posed as bounty hunters and pursued Mark to the town of Ballards Crossing. Here, Mark hoped to find the one man who would believe his story and help to clear his name. But they walked into a town simmering on the brink of an explosive war between the two biggest landowners in the district – Clem Boardman and the beautiful Della Rodriguez.

Caught in the middle, Mark would soon be fighting for his very life.

0121   KINGSTANDING
464 5193   LIBRARY

Loans are up to 28 days. Fines are charged if items are
not returned by the due date. Items can be renewed
at the Library, via the internet or by telephone up to
3 times. Items in demand will not be renewed.
Please use a bookmark

Check out our online catalogue to see what's in stock, or
to renew or reserve books.   - 5 NOV 2014
www.birmingham.gov.uk/libcat
www.birmingham.gov.uk/libraries   1 5 MAY 201

Birmingham City Council

Birmingham
Libraries

Ballards Crossing

Clive Denman

A Black Horse Western

ROBERT HALE · LONDON

© John Glasby 2005
First published in Great Britain 2005

ISBN 0 7090 7842 0

Robert Hale Limited
Clerkenwell House
Clerkenwell Green
London EC1R 0HT

Typeset by
Derek Doyle & Associates, Shaw Heath.
Printed and bound in Great Britain by
Antony Rowe Limited, Wiltshire

CHAPTER 1

BOUNTY HUNT

After hastily kicking dirt on to the embers of the fire, Mark Dalton lay on his stomach with the Winchester pressed hard against his cheek, squinting along it through red-rimmed eyes. The sound he had heard had been distant but in this barren Texas country, a man took note of such small things if he wanted to remain alive.

For six days he had ridden hard through mesquite and brush, across alkali flats with the blistering sun on his back and grit in his eyes. He had forced his mount along narrow switchback trails through the harsh mountain country, crossed stony riverbeds where now only thin trickles of water flowed sluggishly.

All along the way there had been those three bounty hunters on his trail. So far he had succeeded in staying ahead of Seth Tollard and his two companions, sleeping for only a couple of hours each night.

Now they were swiftly catching up with him. He knew

that men like Tollard didn't stop to ask questions; none would be asked as to whether he was innocent or guilty. So long as there was a picture and a reward on some Wanted poster, they would track a man to the ends of the earth.

The fact that he had been framed for the killing of his two friends in Colorado meant nothing to Tollard and the men who rode with him. Once they had him in their sights they would shoot him down and collect the bounty.

Both of the men had been his friends for years, had been gunned down in the street with no chance to defend themselves. Perhaps if he hadn't run out of the saloon and fired those two shots after the fleeing killer, it would have been difficult to pin the killing on him.

Lying there in the darkness, he tried to put his chaotic thoughts into some form of order, to sort out the events of that shooting in his mind. He recalled that Tollard and Cordray had appeared from the other side of the street, claiming that they had seen him fire the shots which had taken his friends in the back. There had been little time for him to think clearly and coherently. When the crowd had gathered, some calling for a lynching, he had made it to his mount and ridden out, knowing it would be impossible to prove his innocence.

Straining his ears, he tried to pick out the sound again, to pinpoint its position, but there was nothing. Only the faint soughing of the breeze among the tall trees disturbed the silence.

The trail lay half a mile away at the bottom of a rocky, tree-lined slope. He had chosen this position carefully, a vantage point from where he could glimpse a narrow portion of the trail through the trees and dense under-growth.

The only chance he had was a slim one. If he could reach Ballards Crossing before these men, the sheriff there, Hal Whitman, had been a friend of his father during the Civil War and he might be the only one who would believe in his innocence.

Shifting himself slightly as cramp tightened the muscles of his legs, he kept his hands tight on the rifle, one finger on the trigger. At this distance, even with a Winchester, it would not be easy to take out three men.

A few yards away the stallion snickered softly, a warning of danger not far away. The previous evening the horse had cast a shoe and he doubted if it could travel far without attention.

The sound came again, louder and nearer, and his trained ears instantly recognized three riders coming forward slowly. It was possible that they had travelled all night and their mounts were tired, but equally it might be that Tollard was taking no chances. He may have guessed he would hole up in a place like this, away from the more open country ahead.

He rubbed his eyes with hard knuckles and tried to ignore the ache in his limbs. Then, ten minutes later, he spotted the three riders. They were moving in single file and he was almost certain he recognized the tall, thin man in the lead as Tollard.

His finger tightened instinctively on the trigger as they passed, one by one, across his narrow field of view. For a moment, he thought they meant to halt. Instead, they rode on and he remained there for several minutes, scarcely daring to breathe.

When a man rode through wild country like this with three killers on his trail, he did not live long if he took any unnecessary chances. After a time, however, he guessed they had decided to ride on to Ballards Crossing, believing that that was where he would make for.

Slowly, he pushed himself to his feet and built himself a smoke. Drawing the smoke deeply into his lungs, he stood quite still, watching as the sky brightened with the coming dawn.

Then, off somewhere in the distance, he heard a gunshot. It was only a single shot but the sharp echo brought him tautly erect. The sound was not repeated and he guessed that one of the men had fired at a shadow, possibly believing it was him.

Not until the sun had risen appreciably among the trees did he make any move. He took the reins and led his mount carefully down the treacherous slope towards the trail, ignoring the persistent ache in his limbs.

Once out in the open, he scanned the terrain, seeing nothing in any direction. In the strengthening sunlight there were fickle overtones in the shadows which lay thickly clustered along part of the trail. About a mile further on, the trail ran through a rocky defile while in the distance, perhaps five miles away, the grasslands began, giving a touch of green to the horizon.

He rode for part of the way, but was eventually forced to step down and walk beside his mount. By now those three men should be well ahead of him unless they had figured he had pulled off the trail somewhere. If that were so, they would be lying in wait for him somewhere close by, where the shadows were deepest.

There was no movement nearby but the apprehension came crowding back on him. Swirling clouds of stinging, abrading dust lifted occasionally in the wind that gusted fitfully from the north-east.

Then a soft sound came from somewhere close by. Frayed nerves and tension made him jerk the Colt from its holster. He dropped to his knees and lowered himself cautiously to the ground, keeping his head down. At any moment he expected a bullet to come at him. When none came, he wriggled forward, then glimpsed the figure lying huddled against a rocky wall, legs thrust out straight in front of him.

Even from that distance, Mark made out the ugly stain of blood on the man's leg. Swiftly, he thrust the Colt back into leather and went forward, standing over the other.

The man lifted a bearded face, pain etched across it. For a moment, the other was silent, then he rasped throatily:

'You come back to make sure I'm dead?'

'I don't aim to kill you,' Mark said evenly. He went down on one knee beside the other. 'Who shot you?'

For an instant, suspicion remained on the grizzled features. Then, hoarsely, the man rasped:

'There were three of 'em. Jumped me as I was ridin' back to my place. Never gave me a chance. One of 'em just pulled a gun and fired.'

'Just lie still and I'll get you some water.' Mark went back to his mount, took down the canteen, brought it back and gave it to the man, who drank greedily.

'Many thanks, mister. Sorry I had you figured for one o' those critters. The name's Sam Casson. I got a small spread about four miles yonder.' He pointed towards the north.

'Mark Dalton.'

The other eyed him shrewdly for a moment.

'If you'll forgive an old man for sayin' so, you got the look of a man on the run.'

Mark gave a terse nod.

'Guess it was me those gunhawks were after. They must've shot you by mistake.'

'Were they the law?'

'Nope. Two of 'em by the names o' Seth Tollard and Pete Cordray had me framed for murder in Colorado. They've been on my tail ever since.'

'That figgers. From what I saw of 'em they sure looked like mean critters, all three of 'em.'

'My guess is they've ridden on to Ballards Crossing. If so, they'll no doubt be waitin' for me.'

Mark took out his knife, slit the leg of the other's pants and examined the wound. He spilt water from the canteen on to his kerchief and wiped away most of the blood.

'Guess you were plumb lucky it didn't hit the bone.' he said at last. 'But you've lost a heap o' blood and the sooner you get a doctor to look at it, the better.'

After binding it up, he leaned forward and grasped the other's hand, pulling him to his feet. Taking his weight on his shoulder, Mark asked:

'You reckon you can ride?'

'If you just give me a help into the saddle. But from what I see, your mount is lame.'

'We'll manage.' With an effort, he helped the other up.

It was almost an hour later when Mark sighted the small spread. There was a ranch house to the north of it with a small dirt courtyard in front.

As they entered the courtyard, the door opened and a woman came out, a rifle in her hands. Mark guessed she was around twenty-five, tall and slim, with long dark hair flowing over her shoulders.

When she saw the man in the saddle, she lowered the rifle and ran forward.

'What happened, Pa?' she asked anxiously. 'I knew something was wrong when you never got back and when those three men rode in asking if any stranger had ridden by, I—'

Mark glanced up sharply at that remark.

'Three men, you say?'

'That's right. Claimed they were lawmen and insisted on searching the whole place. When they found nothing, they rode off towards town.'

'How long ago was that?'

The woman pursed her lips. 'A little over an hour ago.'

Mark nodded but said nothing. He saw the hint of suspicion in her eyes.

'How bad are you hurt, Pa?' she asked.

'He's got a slug in the leg, miss,' Mark said before the other could speak. 'I found him back along the trail aways and guessed he needed help.'

Mark eased the other from the saddle and helped him up as Casson grimaced with pain. Together, Mark and the woman aided him into the house where they sat him in the chair by the window.

The woman glanced at Mark.

11

'I'm Janet Casson,' she said evenly. 'You look as though you've been on the trail a long time.'

'Seems he was framed for killin' two men back in Colorado,' her father put in. 'Those men were bounty hunters.'

'You believe him, Pa?' There was still an expression of indecision and doubt on her features and at the back of the clear grey eyes.

Casson nodded his head.

'I believe him. If he was a killer he'd never have stopped to help me.'

She accepted that.

'Then you're welcome here,' she said. 'I'll make you some breakfast. I doubt if you've eaten a decent meal for days. Then I'll get one of the hands to take a look at your mount. I'll also have to send someone into town for the doctor.'

She went into the kitchen. Casson motioned Mark to a chair.

'I ain't tryin' to poke my nose into your business, Dalton,' he said, 'but where are you headed now? Those men ain't goin' to give up.'

'I've only got one real friend I can trust in this territory. The sheriff in Ballards Crossing knew my father durin' the war.'

'Hal Whitman.'

'You know him?'

'Not had many dealings with him but I hear he's a good man, a straight-shooter. Which is more than can be said for the rest o' that hell-town.'

'Trouble there?' Mark asked.

The other leaned forward a little, easing his leg into

a more comfortable position.

'I've known plenty o' towns along this frontier but that's the worst. Clem Boardman owns a couple o' saloons, backed by his bunch o' killers, and there's Della Rodriguez. She's half-Mexican. Came from somewhere south o' the border about five years ago.'

'Where does she fit in?'

'She owns the biggest spread around here, the Double T. She also runs the Golden Horseshoe saloon. Gambling, dancing-girls, you name it and she has the lot. Boardman has a couple o' smaller saloons on the opposite side o' the street. Heard there's gunplay between the two nearly every night.'

'Sounds as though Whitman has plenty on his hands keepin' law and order in that place,' Mark said.

'Whitman may be a good man but he's gettin' a mite old for that job. Guess that pretty soon he'll be put out to graze and Della will put one of her men in his place.'

At that, Janet came in from the kitchen carrying a plate heaped with bacon, eggs and beans and a mug of hot coffee. She set them down in front of him.

'If you're looking for work,' she said, 'I guess we could do with another hand and—'

'Thanks for the offer, but I have to ride on. Besides, it would be dangerous for you if I was to stay here. Those men will be back and if they suspect that you're hidin' me they wouldn't hesitate to shoot up the place.'

Between mouthfuls, he went on: 'This man Tollard is as mean as a rattler and the two men with him are of the same breed. They shoot first and ask questions later.'

'Then at least you can stay until tomorrow. Doc Cameron is a man who can be trusted. He can tell you if those men are still in town and where they are.'

'Thanks. I'll do that.'

It was two hours later when the doctor arrived. He was a small, grey-haired man with a trim goatee beard. After examining Casson, he said:

'That slug is still in there, Sam. I'll have to take it out. Then I'm afraid you won't be walkin' on that leg for a couple o' days.' He turned to Janet. 'Get me a basin of boiling water and some whiskey,' he said. 'It'll help dull the pain a little.'

'Anythin' I can do to help, Doc?' Mark asked.

The other scrutinized him closely for several seconds. Then he glanced at Casson.

'This the man who brought you back, Sam?'

'That's right. I guess I might have died out there if he hadn't come along.'

'There's talk in town that a killer on the run is headed this way. This wouldn't be him, I presume?'

'You guess right, Doc,' Mark answered. 'Only I ain't no killer.'

'What's your name?'

'Dalton. Mark Dalton. I guess the only one who'll vouch for me is Sheriff Whitman.'

The other shrugged. 'Ain't no concern o' mine if you're a killer or not. Ballards Crossing is full o' gunslingers and killers. But if you're considerin' riding there, you're headin' into big trouble. Most folk give that hell-town a wide berth.'

'So I've heard.' Mark paused, then went on: 'You know anythin' of three men who rode in a little while ago?'

'Sure. Bounty hunters. Can tell 'em a mile away. Is it

you they're lookin' for?'

Mark nodded. 'They trailed me for six days. I managed to give 'em the slip this mornin'. That's when I found Casson. They must've shot him thinkin' he was me in the darkness.'

'Then take my advice. Once you leave here, ride back the way you came. That way, you may stay alive. If not . . .' The other allowed his words to trail away into silence.

'Thanks for the advice, Doc. But those two men who died were my friends. I aim to find out who killed them and make sure he pays. And I've got this gut feelin' that Tollard knows somethin' about it.'

'Reckon that's up to you,' Cameron replied. He made to say something more, then stopped as Janet came in with the basin and a bottle of whiskey.

Cameron pulled up a chair beside Casson and handed him the bottle.

'Take a good slug, Sam.'

While the other gulped the raw liquor the doctor took out his knife and slit more of the material along Casson's leg. The wound had bled a lot but had now stopped.

Clenching his teeth, Casson uttered a low moan deep in his throat as the doctor probed for the bullet. His shoulders jerked and heaved.

'The two of you,' called Cameron. 'Hold him down until I'm finished.'

While Janet held her father's legs, Mark held his shoulders down hard against the chair. Several minutes passed before the doctor said tautly:

'It's out. Now I'll bandage it for you. You were lucky

you got it in the leg instead o' the head.'

Sweat beading his forehead, Casson lay back, staring up at the ceiling. At last he managed to speak.

'Thanks, Doc. And when you go, do me a favour. Don't say a word to anyone about this stranger.'

Cameron pursed his lips, then nodded in acquiescence. 'You must be damned sure of him, Sam. I hope your judgement ain't misplaced.'

'I'll take that chance.'

After the doctor had gone Mark stepped out into the courtyard and made himself a smoke. Over by the small corral he noticed one of the men shoeing his mount. Drawing on his cigarette, he turned things over slowly in his mind.

Stumbling on Casson that morning had been fortunate. At least he had a place of relative safety for a little while. He didn't doubt those bounty hunters were scouring Ballards Crossing for him at that very moment. There was the remote possibility that they had thought he would skirt around the town and ride on to put as much distance as possible between them and himself.

But that was unlikely. Six days on the trail told on any mount. With their own horses almost at the limit of their endurance, being ridden for so long with scarcely any stop, they'd know his own mount would be in the same condition.

He didn't doubt they would remain in Ballards Crossing until they had searched every place where he might hide out. Only then would they begin to consider other possibilities.

There was also the chance they might decide to return to this ranch in their search for him.

A soft footfall at his back caused him to turn sharply and he found that Janet had come out and was standing close behind him. There was a strange expression on her face which he couldn't analyse.

'Why do you have to go on riding into trouble?' she asked at last. 'You'll find nothing else in Ballards Crossing. With my father having that wound in his leg, we need all the help we can get.'

Giving him a direct stare, she continued: 'There are places here where we can hide you if those men do come back. They'll soon tire of searching for you and turn their attention to some other man running from the law.'

He pondered that for a moment. It was certainly a tempting offer. It would mean an end to all this running from one frontier state to another, always looking over his shoulder, never knowing when a gun might spit lead at him from some darkly shadowed alley.

Then he recalled the two friends who had been shot down in the street without a chance of defending themselves, of how Tollard had sworn he had seen him kill them, forcing him to flee before the lynch mob caught up with him. Slowly, he shook his head.

'This is somethin' I have to do. I'll never be a free man until I've hunted down the real killer.'

'I guess I understand but I still think you're a fool. You may get to Sheriff Whitman. But he can't help you. There's no law in that town. From what I've heard, pretty soon a full-scale war will break out between Boardman and Della Rodriguez and there's no one who can stop it. Why ride into the middle of it?'

'Believe me, I don't aim to get into any war. I just figure on gettin' Tollard alone someplace and forcin' the truth out of him.'

'You're just like my father. Stubborn as a goddamn mule.' She turned on her heel and went back into the house.

When he woke next morning it was to find that dark stormclouds had moved in from the distant mountains. Rain slashed against the windows and turned the courtyard into a sea of mud.

He pushed his empty plate away at the breakfast table, sat back and sipped the hot coffee Janet had placed in front of him. Sam Casson had somehow hobbled to the chair by the window and was staring out into the teeming rain. He turned to glance in Mark's direction.

'Ain't no sense in ridin' out right now,' he said sombrely.

'I'm obliged to you for your hospitality but the rain don't bother me none. Ain't the first time I've ridden wet.'

'I weren't thinkin' of the rain,' replied the other. 'But those *hombres* might be watchin' the trail into Ballards Crossing. Much better to try it at night. That way, you might get to the sheriff without bein' seen.'

Mark considered that, then nodded. There was a lot of sense in what Casson suggested. He knew nothing of this town. It would certainly be safer to case it out under cover of darkness. He sat back.

'You ever been bothered by any o' those in Ballards

Crossing?' he asked.

'Not often,' Casson admitted. 'Guess we're too small for them to harass us. Had a few cattle rustled a while back.'

'You got any idea who did it?'

'Sure we know.' Janet had stepped out of the kitchen. Now she stood in the doorway, her arms folded, her face defiant. 'Della Rodriguez.'

'Now we ain't got any proof o' that,' her father admonished. 'For all we know it could've been Boardman's men.'

Janet shook her head vehemently.

'Boardman has also had some of his beef go over the hill from the Circle X spread. I tell you Della Rodriguez wants to take over every ranch in this territory, including Boardman's.'

'That's as maybe,' Sam retorted harshly. 'And if it came to the crunch, I guess I'd sooner see her run out o' this place than Clem Boardman. But from what I've heard, he's got just as many gunslingers as she has and it ain't going to be long afore that whole town blows itself apart in a full-scale range war.'

CHAPTER 2

HELLTOWN

By early evening, the storm had blown itself out, the last of the dark clouds moving swiftly away towards the south-east. A few stars were showing as Mark saddled up and rode out of the ranch. The sun had set an hour earlier and now the moon rose, round and full. From Sam Casson he had learned that Ballards Crossing lay some eight miles away. The railroad ran through it but very few of the trains ever stopped there. Most that did were freights taking cattle to the markets a hundred miles away to the east.

Although it was new to him, the terrain here was little different from that which he had known in Colorado.

The trail ran some half a mile to his left, rising and falling between tall buttes and ragged-edged boulders. On instinct, he had avoided it, taking his mount across rough country where shadows lay thick and innumerable in the brilliant moonlight.

He rode slowly, letting the stallion have its head, sitting tall and easy in the saddle. The utter stillness pressed in on him from all sides; a stillness that held its own overtones of menace.

Off in the distance only the occasional sharp bark of a coyote broke the clinging silence. A moment later it would be repeated from another direction.

An hour passed before he came within sight of Ballard Crossing. A little earlier he had crossed the gleaming metal rails. He reined up and surveyed the town from half a mile away. It was a sprawling place, lying on both sides of a wide street which ran due north and south. The railroad passed through at the southern end and the depot seemed to be the only place in total darkness.

In the centre was a wide square with a few cottonwoods growing. Lying so close to the Mexican border, he guessed there would have been more than a sprinkling of Mexicans there but now that the outlaw bands had moved in, they would be in the minority.

It was probably one of the stops used by mercenary gangs rustling beef across the border. By now, he reckoned, most of the smaller spreads were being squeezed out. It was a scenario he had seen on many occasions in the past.

He touched spurs to the stallion's flanks and drove it forward. In a town like this, he guessed, men rode in all the time and he reckoned that as far as he was concerned only three men would recognize him. To the rest, he would be just another drifter.

He made out three saloons but by far the biggest and grandest had the name The Golden Horseshoe above the entrance.

As he drew his mount into the side near the sheriff's office a sudden burst of gunfire erupted from the far end of the street. A moment later, a bunch of riders came into view, firing their guns into the air.

They brought their mounts to a sliding halt in front of the saloon standing directly opposite the Golden Horseshoe. They tethered their horses to the hitching rail and went inside.

When there was no further disturbance, Mark stepped down, pushed open the door of Whitman's office, and went inside. There was a single lamp on the dust-smeared desk and by its light he made out the grey-haired man seated in the chair.

He guessed the other to be in his late fifties. There was a tired, drawn expression on his face which Mark noticed at once.

'Sheriff Whitman?' he asked softly.

Lifting his head, Whitman eyed the man in front of him, noticing the Colts sitting low at his waist. From the look of him, he reckoned this was a man who knew how to use them.

He nodded his head with a trace of a frown on his face.

'That's right, stranger,' he said. 'I hope you ain't in town lookin' for trouble.'

'I never look for trouble, Sheriff, but if it starts, I sure as hell finish it.'

Whitman sighed audibly as he leaned back.

'Another gunhawk. I guessed it. What's your business in Ballards Crossing?'

'I came lookin' for you,' Mark said, leaning across the desk. 'I need your help.'

Surprise showed on the other's lined features.

'You want my help? And what can I. . . ?' Whitman broke off and stared hard at Mark, a curious expression in his eyes. For a moment, he seemed at a loss for words. Then he said wonderingly: 'You got the look of . . .'

'Cal Dalton?'

'Why yes, but . . .' He came quickly to his feet. 'You Cal Dalton's son, Mark?'

'Thats right. I gather you fought together in the war.'

'You're danged right we did.' Reaching forward, Whitman grasped Mark's hand and shook it vigorously. 'Hellfire, I never expected to see you here in this hell-town.' His tone changed abruptly, became more serious. 'But you say you want my help.'

Mark seated himself.

'I was framed for the murder o' my two partners in Colorado,' he began. 'Now there are three bounty hunters on my tail. I managed to throw 'em off a couple o' days back but my guess is they're here in Ballards Crossing.'

'You don't need to ask if I believe you're innocent, Mark,' said the sheriff sincerely. 'Just who are these men?'

'Seth Tollard is their leader. The other two are gunhawks in it for the reward money, Ned Randers and Pete Cordray. They trailed me for six days before I got help from a rancher and his daughter.'

Whitman rubbed his chin.

'Sam Casson and Janet. Funny they'd help a stranger. Their place has been hit once or twice by rustlers.'

'I came upon the old man on the trail. Tollard or one o' the others shot him, probably thinkin' it was me. I managed to get him back to the ranch.'

'Guess that explains it.' Whitman took out a cigar, lit it and blew smoke into the air. Scratching his cheek, he went on: 'Guess if you're to stay in town you'll need some place to hide out from these bounty hunters. Won't be any use goin' over to the hotel, that'll be the first place they'll look, if they haven't been there already.'

'Can you think of any other place? I'm hopin' those three are still in town. I aim to get Tollard on his own if I can. There are some mighty important questions I want to ask him and when I do, it'll be at the point of a gun.'

'Guess there's one place they won't think o' looking,' Whitman said at last. 'At the top o' the livery stables. Only feed there for the horses and I guess I can get food to you. I'll try to find out more about these three *hombres* who're chasin' you.'

'Thanks.' Mark sat back, listening to the noise outside in the street. 'A bunch o' men came into town just as I rode in, shootin' off their guns. Who were they?'

Whitman snorted. 'Some o' Boardman's crowd, I reckon. It happens almost every night. Just so long as they don't start any killin', I let it go. Ain't much I could do about it anyways. There's no real law in Ballards Crossing now. All I can do is try to keep a lid on any range war that could break out at any time between Boardman and Della Rodriguez.'

In the darkness at the rear of the livery stables, Mark just made out the ladder resting against the wide ledge which stretched the entire width of the building. In spite of all the activity going on in town, Whitman had led him around the rear of the buildings without his being seen.

'You'll be quite safe up there,' the sheriff murmured in a low voice. 'I'll come by in the mornin' with some grub. In the meantime, I'll keep my eyes and ears open. See if I can find out anythin' about this Seth Tollard and his sidekicks.'

Mark stood poised with one foot on the lowest rung.

'Thanks for doin' this for me.'

'Anythin' for Cal Dalton's son. Your pa saved my life once and I ain't ever goin' to forget it. Just be careful if you decide to move around town. You may not realize it but all strangers who ride into Bollards Crossing are watched by everybody. Sooner or later, either Clem Boardman or Della Rodriguez gets to know and that's when trouble can start, big trouble.'

'I'll be careful,' Mark promised.

He waited until the other had stepped out of the shadows into the street, then made his way slowly up the ladder. At times, he felt sure the wood was going to snap under his weight but somehow he made it to the top, where he threw himself down on to the hay.

Music and noise still came from the saloons along the street. Once or twice he heard the sharp crack of a gunshot. Whether someone had just died, or this was the way the riders let off steam, he didn't know. But Casson and Whitman had not exaggerated when they had described Ballards Crossing as a hell-town, he mused as he stared into the darkness.

He had passed through almost a score of frontier

towns like this, towns which had sprung up and were now in their death throes. Killing and violence always accompanied the building of these places.

Sometimes, they destroyed themselves in the ferocity of a range war. Only a few managed to enter into a period of some kind of law and order and it was those which would grow and flourish.

An hour passed. Still the din continued. It was well after midnight before he picked out the sound of horses passing the stables, heading out of town. The tinny sound of piano music became more intermittent.

He took off his gunbelt and laid it beside him, then stretched out and closed his eyes.

How long he slept it was impossible to tell. It was still dark when he woke abruptly.

Something, some faint sound had seeped into that part of his mind which never slept and woken him with a warning of imminent danger. Very slowly he eased himself into a sitting position, hefting the Colt into his hand. With every sense alert, he tried to determine the source of the noise which had brought him awake.

For a moment, the darkness and the silence were absolute. Then the sound came again, a furtive movement almost directly below him, near the long row of stalls. One of the horses snickered softly.

Making no sound, he eased himself forward until he could see over the lip of the wide ledge. Narrowing his eyes, he made out the shapes of two men standing close to the stall where his own mount was tethered.

In the dimness it was impossible to discern the men's faces, but a moment later one of them spoke in low tones. He immediately recognized Seth Tollard.

'I tell you this is his mount, I'd recognize it anywhere. He's somewhere in town.'

'Well, he ain't in the hotel, that's for sure.'

Mark made out Ned Randers's harsh tones. Straining his vision, he could see no sign of the third member of the gang.

'You're sure he talked with the sheriff?'

'Sure. I saw 'em both through the window. Seemed to be havin' quite a conversation.'

There ensured a long silence, then Tollard muttered:

'You reckon that somehow he knows it was you who shot those two men?'

'If he does, he knows too damned much. Somehow, I reckon that sheriff knows where he is. Shouldn't be too difficult to get that old man to talk.'

Mark eased the Colt forward and felt his finger tighten instinctively on the trigger. Then sanity prevailed and he forced himself to ease off the pressure. No sense shooting down these two men. Even though he now knew who had murdered his partners, and framed him for the killing, it wouldn't be easy to prove it.

Killing them both now would only land him in bigger trouble. Cordray was still around somewhere and he would swear he had shot them in cold blood. Even Whitman would be unable to help him then.

Remaining absolutely still, he waited. He saw Tollard move forward a little way towards the ladder, resting his hand on one of the lower rungs. For a moment, Mark thought he intended to climb up but then the other leaned back, rolled a smoke and lit it with a sulphur match.

'What I don't figure is why he headed here,' Randers said harshly. 'Ain't as if he knows anybody here who could help him.'

'Unless he's in cahoots with the sheriff.'

Tollard uttered a harsh laugh.

'If he expects the law to help him, he's ridin' the wrong trail. I've been askin' around and the only law in this town is Della Rodriguez. She ain't the sort o' woman to take kindly to strangers but I reckon if we were to explain the position she might help find him. Seems there ain't much goes on in Ballards Crossing she don't know about.'

'Guess she might do that if we were to offer her half the reward money,' Randers suggested. 'Wherever he's holed up, there ain't no sense lookin' for him tonight.'

There was no further conversation and a little while later the two men sauntered out of the stables and vanished around the corner. Lying there, Mark recalled the threat in Randers's voice when he had mentioned Hal Whitman.

Men like Randers and Tollard knew ways of making men talk, and where they were concerned life was cheap. It mattered little if the person under interrogation died just so long as they got the information they wanted.

Somehow he had to warn Whitman before these men got to him. There was a grim tautness in him as he climbed down to the stalls after buckling on his gunbelt. He padded to the door and risked a quick look along the street in both directions. Nothing moved in the moonthrown shadows. Everywhere seemed deserted.

Moving silently along the boardwalk, he passed two stores in darkness. In front of him was the Golden Horseshoe saloon and here he paused. A light was still visible, showing faintly above the batwing doors. Cautiously, he peered inside.

For a moment he could see no one. The light came from a single lantern at the end of the long, polished bar. Then, almost out of sight, he made out the two figures.

Tollard and Randers!

Pressing himself tightly against the wall, he waited. There was something going on here which he didn't understand. A few moments later, a door at the back of the stage opened and a woman came through.

One glimpse was sufficient to tell Mark that this was not one of the usual dancing-girls. This woman had an aristocratic bearing with raven hair flowing over her shoulders and beautiful, but hard, features.

Although he had never seen her before, he knew instantly who she was. Della Rodriguez, owner of the Golden Horseshoe and one of the biggest and most powerful landowners in the territory. She took down a bottle from the shelf behind her and placed it in front of the two men.

Puzzled, Mark watched as she engaged Tollard and Randers in deep conversation. Evidently the two men had wasted no time, possibly taking the chance that she might still be there, checking on the night's takings.

Some instinct told him that the topic of their conversation could well be himself. There was that $5,000 reward for his capture, dead or alive. It was quite possible that this was the kind of money Della would be interested in if she was to gain the upper hand on Clem Boardman.

Knowing it would be impossible to make out anything of what they were saying, Mark lowered his head as he passed across the doors. He had no idea where Whitman might be at that hour. He might have a room at the hotel, or possibly sleep in the jailhouse.

There was no light in the window of his office. Everything was quiet and in darkness. He knocked softly on the door and waited, his right hand close to the gun at his waist.

A couple of minutes passed, then he picked out the soft sound footsteps. The door opened slightly. Whitman's puzzled face peered through the opening.

'Sorry if I woke you, Hal, but this is important.'

'Mark! I thought I left you at the livery stables. Somethin' happened?'

Swiftly, Mark went inside and closed the street door behind him.

'I was wakened there by voices. Tollard and Randers. I heard enough to know it was Randers who shot those two men.

'Tollard recognized my mount and they know I'm somewhere in town. Randers said he knew ways of makin' you tell them where I was holed up.'

'Where are those two critters now?' WHitman asked.

'You ain't gonna believe this. They're in the Golden Horseshoe deep in conversation with Della Rodriguez.'

Mark heard the other's intake of breath at this news.

'You're sure o' that?'

'I'm sure. Tall, black-haired Mexican woman.'

In the dimness he saw the other's affirmative nod.

'That's Della all right.' Whitman scratched his chin. 'But that makes no sense. I ain't ever seen any of those men before. How come she knows them?' He made to light the lamp on the desk but Mark stopped him.

'Better not show a light, Hal. There could be eyes watchin'.'

'Good thinkin',' Whitman agreed.

In the darkness they seated themselves on either side of the desk.

'Either they know each other from way back,' Mark said, 'or more likely, they've told Della about the reward money for my capture. Guess she may be willin' to get her boys to hunt me down for a share of it.'

Whitman chewed that over for a moment.

'Either way, it means you're in danger here.'

'I've had men on my trail before, includin' those three. If they want to start trouble, I won't stop 'em.'

Whitman leaned forward, his elbows on the desk.

'That's easily said, Mark. But you can't go up against all the men Della has at her beck and call. Only one man in town big enough to do that: Clem Boardman, and he'd probably think twice about it.'

His tone serious, the sheriff went on: 'You'd better think about this. I wouldn't like to see you in Boot Hill just because you're intent on showin' you're a better man than all the others. Like I told you, this is a hell-town and there are plenty who'd shoot you in the back if Della gave the order. Then Tollard would just sit back and collect that reward. Is that what you want?'

'If you're suggestin' I fork my mount and ride out, that's somethin' I can't do, Hal. I'd spend the rest o' my life lookin' over my shoulder, never findin' a place where I could put down my roots.'

The other threw up his hands in exasperation, made to say something. Then Mark thrust out an arm, grabbed Whitman's wrist and motioned him to silence.

They both heard the faint sound almost immediately outside the street door. Mark rose silently from his chair and crossed the room into the short passage leading to the cells, his Colt already in his hand. Now that his eyes had become accustomed to the gloom, he could make out everything clearly.

There was the sound of breathing and the door-handle turned quietly. A thin shaft of yellow moonlight spilled into the room. Through the widening crack, a dark shadow fell across it as the man edged silently inside.

The intruder must have seen Whitman almost at once for he stepped quickly inside, closing the door. There was a gun in his hand, pointed directly at the sheriff as he thrust himself over the desk.

'Don't make a sound or any move I don't like, Sheriff. I'm here for information and you're goin' to give it to me.'

With a faint sense of surprise Mark realized that the other was neither Tollard or Randers. It was Pete Cordray.

'Information about what?' Whitman asked gratingly.

'Where I can find Mark Dalton. I know he's in town and I also know you've talked to him. Now where is he?'

'Right behind you, Cordray.' Mark thrust the barrel of his Colt hard into the other's back. 'Now drop that gun or you're a dead man.'

He felt the other stiffen. For a moment, he thought

that Cordray was going to make a play. Then, reluctantly, Cordray released his hold on the Colt. Whitman picked it up as the gunhawk let it fall on to the desk.

'Now before we lock you up in one o' the cells, I suggest you do some talkin' yourself.' Prodding Cordray viciously in the back, Mark forced him towards the chair.

'You're in no position to ask questions, Dalton. There's a warrant out for you, dead or alive.'

Mark laughed thinly.

'Yeah. For two murders that Randers committed. I overheard your two friends talkin' in the livery stables less than half an hour ago.'

Mark saw at once that the shot had gone home. 'Guess once the federal marshal hears o' this, you'll all be swingin' on the end of a rope.'

'You don't reckon you'll reach a federal marshal alive, do you? You'll never leave this town.'

'Now why should you think that?' Mark forced evenness into his tone. 'Sheriff Whitman here believes me. That makes it two guns against three unless' – he leaned forward, pushing his face up to the other's – 'you're tyin' yourselves in with Della Rodriguez, givin' her a share o' the reward in return for sendin' her gunslicks after me.'

'Who the hell is Della Rodriguez? I ain't never heard of her.'

It was clear from Cordray's tone that he was lying.

'You know damn well who she is,' Mark snapped. 'Both o' your friends are talkin' to her in the Golden Horseshoe right now.'

'I ain't sayin' anything,' Cordray growled.

33

Mark straightened, still keeping the other covered.

'Better lock him up in one o' the cells for the night, Hal, we can decide what to do with him in the mornin'.'

Whitman took down a bunch of keys from the wall and led the way along the short passage. He opened a cell door and waited while Mark thrust Cordray inside. Then he locked it again.

'If you reckon you can hold me here, you're mistaken,' Cordray called as they walked away.

'We'll see about that,' Mark replied harshly.

Back in the office, Whitman took out a bottle and two glasses. He deliberately kept the place in darkness.

Sipping his drink, the lawman said soberly:

'He's right, you know. Once Della Rodriguez hears o' this and comes ridin' in with her boys, I'll have to let him go. This town is shelterin' a whole nest o' rattlers and it's liable to blow up in my face at any minute.'

Mark regarded him for a while through the faint haze of tobacco smoke.

'Let him go when the time comes. I'll be ready for him and the others.' He paused for a moment, then went on: 'What's this man Boardman like?'

'Clem? Like most o' the others, he's a killer. He didn't get where he is now by just relyin' on others and he's fast with a gun. His spread, the Circle X, joins on to Della's and there's been talk of rustlin' in both directions across their boundaries.'

'Then I guess they aren't the best o' friends.'

'If either thought they could win out without losin' too much, they'd start a war right now. As things are, they're about evenly matched.'

Whitman finished his drink and poured himself

another. Staring at Mark over the rim of his glass, he asked:

'You ain't thinkin' of throwing in your lot with Boardman, are you? Sure, you'd get some protection from Della and these bounty hunters but that would be a fool thing to do.'

'Why? Seems I have no other choice if I want to stay alive long enough to bring Randers to justice and clear my name.'

Mark poured more of the liquor into his glass.

'Well . . .' The other seemed momentarily at a loss for words. At last he said:

'He's a born killer for one thing. If he gets his way, he'll take over everything.'

Mark shrugged. 'Seems to me that nearly everyone in this town is a killer, either workin' for Boardman or Della Rodriguez.'

'Guess there's some sense in what you say.' Whitman agreed. 'But don't underestimate Boardman. Once you sign up with him it ain't goin' to be easy to pull out. Nobody walks out on him.'

'Sometimes a man has to choose between two evils. I'll make sure I get out when the time is right. Where would I find Boardman?'

'Take the trail at the far end o' town. About a mile along it, the track forks. The left trail goes west to Della's place. You take the other and it'll bring you to the Circle X. It's about twelve miles.'

'Thanks,' Mark said, getting to his feet.

In the darkness, he saw the faint gust of surprise on the sheriff's face.

'You aim to ride out now?'

'I figure that might be best. This town is goin' to be mighty unhealthy for me if Della's men come ridin' in to bust Cordray out o' jail. I'll take my time. I should hit Boardman's place around dawn.'

'All right, if you've made up your mind. But ride careful. Boardman's no fool and he knows that Della could hit him at any time. As sure as hell, there'll be men watchin' that trail.'

Mark came upon the fork in the trail less than an hour later. He had seen no one as he made his way along the street to the stables and this time the Golden Horseshoe had been in complete darkness. Evidently the two bounty hunters had finished their business with Della Rodriguez.

Total silence now closed down on him. There was still light by which to make out his surroundings although the moon was sinking slowly towards the west.

Half a mile further on the trail began to climb the irregular slopes of a long plateau which rose sharply from the flatness of the plain. At frequent intervals now his mount slowed, knowing its own pace; with no real urgency in his mind he allowed it to do so.

There was a chill wind blowing down from the plateau, scouring his face and tugging at his jacket. Above his head, the stars were brilliant.

After a little while he reined up and rolled himself a smoke, shielding his cigarette with his jacket against the wind as he lit it. He didn't want to ride on to Boardman's spread in the darkness. That would be asking for trouble.

Anyone watching this trail was likely to shoot first if a

stranger rode up in the darkness.

Not until the dawn was brightening in the east did he push the stallion forward in the direction of the broad grasslands and tree-covered slopes which now showed on the horizon.

The large herd was just stirring itself to his right when a harsh voice rang out from somewhere just within the fringe of trees.

'Hold it right there, mister and keep your hands away from those guns.'

Jerking hard on the reins, Mark brought the stallion to a sudden halt, his hands well clear of the Colts. A moment later, two men stepped into view. Both had Winchesters trained on him.

Thin-lipped, the man who had spoken said:

'This is Boardman territory.' He walked forward and gripped the reins of Mark's horse. The other man kept him covered.

'So I understand,' Mark replied evenly. 'I came to see if Clem Boardman is lookin' for any more hired hands.'

The other's eyes narrowed to mere slits. He turned his head to glance at his companion.

'You recognize this *hombre*, Slim?'

The other shook his head. 'Nope. Never seen him before,' he muttered. 'Reckon I know most o' Della's men and he ain't one of 'em.'

The first man evidently made up his mind at that.

'All right, friend. Just move ahead of me. One move I don't like and you'll get a bullet. Got that?'

Mark nodded and edged the stallion along the narrow trail. As he rounded a bend, he came within sight of the ranch house. Eyeing it closely, he could see that Boardman had certainly done very well for himself. The building was in the old colonial style with a porch and veranda stretching the whole way along the front.

Mark slid easily from the saddle and waited.

Suddenly the door swung open and a man stood there, almost filling the opening. He looked down at Mark with a flat, curious stare: a big man with piercing blue eyes that took in every detail.

He stepped down into the courtyard and planted himself directly in front of the stallion.

'He was ridin' along the trail by the east pasture on the road from town, Mr Boardman,' the man beside Mark said harshly. 'Reckons he's lookin' for a job.'

A faint smile appeared on Boardman's lips.

'You must be either a fool or a very brave man,' he said. His gaze was hard and appraising as if a little unsure what to make of Mark.

'At the moment, I'm not quite sure about that myself,' Mark replied, holding the other's steady gaze.

'You're a stranger in Ballards Crossing. I don't recollect havin' seen you before.'

'Rode in only a couple o' days ago.'

'No doubt with the law on your tail,' Boardman said with a touch of dryness in his tone.

Mark shook his head.

'Not exactly, but there are three bounty hunters after me. One of 'em killed my two partners and then framed me for it.'

Boardman thought that over, then said:

'Ain't no concern o' mine whether you killed those men or not. Most everyone in Ballards Crossing has killed someone, whether in self-defence or that was the way they was born.'

'Then you'd be willin' to give me a job?'

'I always need men I can trust, men fast with a gun whenever the necessity arises. Can you handle those guns you're wearin'?'

'If I have to,' Mark answered evenly.

Boardman considered that, remaining briefly silent. Then he gave a terse nod.

'All right. You're hired. Chet here will show you where you can put your mount and then the bunkhouse.'

Without another word, Boardman turned on his heel and went back into the house. Chet stepped forward.

'This way,' he said. 'I'm Chet Stebbins. The other man you met on the trail is Slim Hallam. You'll find that if you're workin' for Boardman you're safe from any lawmen who might come ridin' this way. Reckon all of us here are on the run from somethin' or someone.'

Breakfast was ready ten minutes later in the bunkhouse. Having found a seat at the long table, Mark ate ravenously. The food was good and it was clear that Boardman treated his men well.

Beside him, Stebbins wiped his mouth with the back of his hand. 'Why's you decide to work for the boss? Most o' the men who ride this way go over to Della Rodriguez.'

'Who's she?' Mark asked, feigning ignorance.

For a moment there was a hint of something at the back of the other's eyes.

'How long you been in Ballards Crossing?'

'A couple o' days.'

'She has the spread next to this. Always havin' trouble with her men rustlin' our beef.'

One of the other men seated opposite Mark spoke up.

'We lost four of our boys a few nights ago in town. Her men started a gunfight outside the saloon. The next time, we'll be ready for 'em.'

'And when will the next time be?' Mark asked.

'Tonight. We ride in tonight,' Stebbins answered. 'You'll be ridin' with us. That way, the boss will find out if you really are any good with those guns.'

CHAPTER 3

ERUPTION OF VIOLENCE

Whitman was standing outside his office the next morning, chewing on the end of a cigar, when the bunch of riders approached from the far end of the street. Stiffly, he jerked himself away from the rail as he recognized Della Rodriguez in the lead.

Remaining in the saddle, she spoke haughtily.

'I understand you have a friend of mine locked up in your jail, Sheriff.'

Whitman tossed the cigar butt into the street.

'I got one man locked up,' he admitted. 'Says his name is Cordray. Stranger in town.'

'What's the charge against him?'

Whitman forced himself to meet the hard stare of her black eyes.

'He forced his way into my office early this mornin' and held me up at gunpoint,' he said. 'Started askin' me a lot o' questions, threatenin' me with the gun. As the elected law in this town, reckon that gives me the right to toss him into one o' the cells.'

'What sort of questions was he asking?' Della demanded in a tone which brooked no denial.

Whitman hesitated, inwardly debating how much to tell. Della leaned forward and took the horsewhip from where it lay close to the saddle.

'I've whipped men before when they don't answer me,' she said through tightly clenched teeth.

Whitman flinched, knowing she meant every word. Swallowing, he said hoarsely:

'He told me he was some kind o' bounty hunter. He and two others had trailed some man to Ballards Crossing. He wanted to know if I'd seen him.'

'And. . . ?'

'I tried to tell him I knew nothin' of this man but he wouldn't believe me.'

A cruel smile twisted Della's bright-red lips.

'And I don't believe you either.'

'But I—'

'Who else was in your office at the time?'

'Why, no one.'

'You're lying, Whitman. A bounty hunter, a common gunslinger, holds you up at gunpoint, yet somehow you manage to disarm him and put him in the cells. An old man like you.'

She turned to Tollard, sitting his mount beside her. 'Go and get your friend out,' she said sharply. 'I'm sure once we've done that we can make the good sheriff talk and tell us where this *hombre* Dalton is hiding out.'

Tollard dismounted and went into the office. A few moments later he emerged with Cordray close on his heels. Cordray had collected his gun and now he thrust it hard into Whitman's ribs.

'The next time you pull a stunt like that, I'll kill you. In fact I ought to kill you right now and—'

'Put that gun away.' Della's words struck across the silence like sparks. 'I'll do all the killing here if I think it's necessary.'

Reluctantly, Cordray lowered the gun, then pushed it into its holster.

'Now,' Della's tone was deceptively soft but menacing, 'I want to know where Dalton is and you're going to tell me.'

'I don't know,' Whitman said harshly. 'Sure he was in the office early this mornin'. He wanted a place to hide until these bounty hunters gave up lookin' for him.'

'And where did you tell him to conceal himself?'

'At the top o' the livery stables. Far as I know that's where he is now.'

Della's right hand barely moved as she gave a flick of her wrist. The whip snaked out, the tip drawing a bloody line down Whitman's cheek. He staggered back against the wall and put up a hand, stared down at the blood on his fingers.

'I'll ask you again. Where did you tell him to go?'

'I've already told you. He—'

Again, the whip flicked out, etching a red weal along the sheriff's other cheek.

'Could be he's tellin' the truth, Della,' Tollard said. 'Me and Randers were in the stables before we went along to the saloon. Dalton's mount was there all right. I recognized it right away.'

Della turned her gaze on him, a scornful expression

in her eyes.

'But you didn't think to search the place, even know-ing it would be the last place anyone would look.'

'Guess we figured he wouldn't be so stupid as to hide in the same place as his mount.' Randers spoke up for the first time.

'So now he could be anywhere in the territory.' Anger thinned the woman's voice.

'Wherever he is, he won't be far away,' Cordray put in. Della stared down at him.

'What makes you so sure of that?' she demanded.

'He was in the stables when Tollard and Randers were talkin'. He heard Randers admit he did the killin'. When they locked me in the cells, he swore he was goin' to bring Randers to justice if it was the last thing he did.'

'Then he's still around here someplace,' Della said. Turning slightly to face Tollard, she went on: 'You check the livery stable. If his mount is still there, some-one's hiding him in town and it won't take long to find out who. If not, he's probably out in the hills. But he'll come back and when he does, we'll get him.'

She lowered her burning gaze to Whitman. 'You know a lot more than you're saying, Sheriff. If I find you're in this with him, you'll regret it.'

She wheeled her mount and sent it racing along the street, signalling to the others to follow. The cloud of white dust settled slowly in their wake.

Whitman took out his kerchief and dabbed at the blood on his face, cursing softly under his breath. He felt humiliated, knowing that several of the townsfolk had been watching events.

He hoped that by now Mark had reached the Circle

X ranch and joined up with Clem Boardman. With Della just as determined as those three bounty hunters to track him down, it was the only place of safety for him in the territory.

Certainly, if Boardman knew that Della was so desperate to get her hands on him, he would never hand him over to her.

Ballards Crossing was its usual wild and noisy self when Mark rode in with six of Boardman's men that evening. Inwardly, he disliked what he felt was sure to happen, this test which Boardman had laid on him. He knew the men riding with him were there to exact revenge for the shooting of their companions.

But the fact that he knew none of her men, had never come face to face with them in his life, grated with him. True, he had shot several men in the past but always in self-defence. In a subtle way, this was different.

Certainly, if trouble started, those men would be just as determined to kill him. In a town like this, life meant little and only the man who was fastest with the gun survived.

'Just watch your back, Mark, once we hit the saloon,' Hallam said. 'There are sure to be plenty o' Della's men in town and there could be others who've got a grudge against the boss.'

'I'll be careful.'

'And we don't want to lose any more men. If we can down a few o' Della's boys, it'll even things up a bit.'

Mark felt a little shiver pass through him at the callousness in the other's tone. Casson had not lied when he had described this as the worst kind of town. Sooner or later, it was going to burst wide open in an orgy of killing and feuding.

He dismounted outside the Trail's End saloon and followed the other men inside. As he passed through the doors, he threw a swift glance over his shoulder towards the Golden Horseshoe across the street. His keen gaze caught sight of the two men who had been lounging on the boardwalk just outside, seemingly taking little notice of what was going on. Now they turned sharply and sidled into the lights and music of Della's place.

The saloon was crowded as Mark stepped inside. Sidling up to Stebbins at the bar, he spoke quietly.

'Our arrival's been noticed, Chet. A couple of men just went inside the Golden Horseshoe. I reckon we should be ready.'

With a grim twist to his lips, the other replied:

'We're ready whenever they decide to make their play.' He called to the bartender and Mark splashed the whiskey into the glass in front of him.

Since this saloon belonged to Boardman, he doubted if any trouble would come from the men inside. He took two swallows of the liquor.

From behind him, he heard the doors swing open. He flicked a quick glance into the mirror behind the bar, then stiffened. The two men who entered he recognized instantly.

Tollard and Cordray!

There was no sign of Randers but Mark guessed he would not be far away.

'That was pretty smart o' you, lining up with Boardman,' Tollard said. 'Won't do you any good. Now, either you see sense and come quietly or we take you with us over the back of a horse.'

Beside Mark, the other riders turned slowly.

'These two o' the bounty hunters you mentioned?' Hallam said softly.

'That's right.' Mark turned and moved away from the counter. He saw Cordray step sideways until he was separated from his companion by several feet. It was an old move. When one went for the draw, the other would do likewise, hoping to take him from a different direction.

'Reckon you two *hombres* are in the wrong place,' Hallam said coldly. 'This man is ridin' with us now. If you want to take on all seven of us, you're welcome to try.'

'No!' There was an edge of sharpness to Mark's tone. 'These aren't Della's riders even if they are in some kind o' deal with her. This is my fight. If they start anythin', I'll finish it.'

Cordray uttered a coarse laugh. He stared at Mark with eyes that never blinked.

'Reckon we're goin' to have to take you the hard way.'

'Reckon you are.' Now that he was face to face with them, Mark knew that this could end only in one way. His gaze flicked across to Tollard. 'You don't seem too sure of yourself,' he said coldly. 'These men here ain't goin' to take any part in this. But it seems to me you need your friend here to back your play.'

A glare of hatred showed on Tollard's face at this implied insult as he slowly drew back his frock-coat a little, exposing the Colt low on his hip. 'I've killed better men than you, Dalton,' he hissed. 'Men who thought they were fast with a gun.'

'There's always a first time.'

Tollard's swarthy features were working under the wide-brimmed hat and Mark noticed a faint sheen of sweat on his forehead, trickling down the sides of his face.

A few yards away, Cordray held himself ready. His right hand hung low over the handle of the Colt. His thin lips were twisted into a sneering grin.

Taking a further step forward, Mark deliberately unfocused his gaze so that he could make out both men at the same time, ready for any move either of them made. Then Tollard turned slightly as if to walk out of the saloon.

As if it had been a prearranged signal, both men went for their guns. They were fast, dangerously fast, but in a single blur of motion, Mark's hands moved. The twin Colts seemed to jump from their holsters. Three shots rang out deafeningly inside the saloon.

Near the door, Cordray was slumping forward, lifting himself on his toes as if to fling himself at Mark. He was dead on his feet, eyes wide and staring in shock. Legs buckling, he slammed into one of the tables, splintering it beneath his weight.

The single shot that Tollard had fired kicked a spurt of dust from the floor near his feet. The gun fell from his hand and his right arm went up as if clutching at something near the ceiling. He remained upright for a long moment, fighting savagely to hold life in his body.

Reaching out, his left hand clawed at a nearby table for support. Then he went down, dragging it with him.

Very slowly, Mark thrust the guns back into their holsters. Beside him, Hallam spoke in an awestruck tone,

'Hellfire, I ain't never seen anythin' like that.'

Tightening his lips, Mark said:

'There's still one of 'em around somewhere. From what I overheard, he's the real killer and they pinned the rap on me.'

'You goin' to kill him if you find him?'

'Nope. I want him alive. Somehow, I'm goin' to make him talk.'

Hallam shrugged. 'It's your fight. Guess that's entirely up to you.'

Mark turned back to the bar. He'd had no compunction in shooting those two men. In the past when he had come up against men who had forced him to draw, there had been nothing personal in it.

Men called each other out all the time in these frontier towns, often just to see who was the fastest with a gun. But killing Cordray and Tollard had been an act of revenge. Even though neither man had pulled the trigger that had killed his friends, they had clearly been in it with Randers.

Hoping to take his mind off these morbid thoughts he turned to Stebbins.

'How many o' Della's men do you reckon are in the Golden Horseshoe?' he asked.

Stebbins scratched his chin, then muttered:

'Twenty or thirty, I'd imagine.'

Mark's stare was one of incredulity.

'Twenty or thirty? And you ride in here with only six? That's plumb crazy.'

Stebbins's lips curled into a grim smile.

'Not really.' He jerked a thumb towards the rest of the men in the saloon. 'Boardman's no fool. Neither are we. Those boys rode into town in twos and threes durin' the afternoon. Reckon that other crew are in for a nasty surprise when they decide to ride out.'

'How long before that happens?'

'When they're good and ready, I guess.' There was a

relaxed nonchalance in Stebbins's tone as he finished his drink and poured himself another.

From the easy attitude of the men in the saloon Mark guessed it would be some time before they made their move. Leaning his elbows on the bar, he followed Stebbins's example but drank the whiskey more slowly.

An hour passed, then two. At the end of that time, several of the men got up from the tables and along the bar and made for the door in small groups. Watching them, Mark guessed they were making for their places along the street, ready for when Della's men left.

An unaccustomed tightness knotted the muscles of his stomach as he finished his last drink. This was something he had never guessed he was letting himself in for when he had ridden into Ballards Crossing. He felt like a rat being forced into a corner.

Those men in the other saloon were all strangers to him. Just the fact that they were hired by Della Rodriguez meant that he would have to kill some of them. Then he recalled what he had seen earlier in the Golden Horseshoe and heard from Cordray in the sheriff's office. Wishing to get her hands on some of that reward money out for him, Della had given orders to her men to hunt him down and kill him.

He jerked himself away from the bar as Hallam touched his arm and turned to follow them outside. Apart from a couple of hobos making their way unsteadily along the boardwalk near the hotel and a large bunch of horses tied up some fifty yards away, the street appeared deserted.

Wherever the rest of Boardman's men were, they had concealed themselves well. Moving silently, keeping well into the dark shadows, they made their way close to where the Double T horses were tethered.

From along the street the din inside the Golden Horseshoe was diminishing slowly. The sound of the tinny piano dwindled as if the pianist had drunk too much and was falling asleep on his stool.

A couple of riders emerged into the street, swaying slightly. Both had Colts in their hands and began shooting into the air. More followed, turning in the direction of their mounts.

The leading group was some thirty yards from Mark when Hallam deliberately stepped out into the street.

'I figure you lot have some reckonin' coming,' he called loudly.

The men stopped. Something about the utter stillness and this one man standing there must have hit them.

'That you, Hallam?' called one of the men at the front. He uttered a harsh laugh. 'You figurin' on takin' us all on like those others?'

'That was where you make a big mistake,' Hallam answered. 'Now it's payback time.'

'Like hell it is,' snarled the other. Before he finished speaking, his right hand dropped towards his gun, jerked it free of leather.

Instantly, Hallam threw himself sideways, firing from the hip as he went down.

The man staggered, clutched at his chest, then went down.

Rolling over, Hallam threw himself beside Mark. Then everything was drowned out in the racketing din of gunfire. Slugs chopped pieces of wood from the trough near Mark's head as he threw two shots into the milling crowd of men.

Caught from both sides as men poured from the alleys, Della's men ran for the dubious cover of the opposite boardwalk. Three broke away and raced for the saloon.

Two swayed and went down before they had covered half the distance. The third, throwing wild shots over his shoulder, reached the door just before a bullet got him in the back. Throwing out his arms, he clutched at the swing-doors, hung there for a moment before they gave way under his weight, pitching him inside.

From the way the man lay there, his legs thrust out on to the boardwalk, Mark knew that the slug had found its target. Moments later, the gunfire from across the street ceased abruptly.

Then a harsh voice yelled:

'You ain't goin' to get away with this, Hallam. You're all backin' a loser if you reckon Boardman can stand up against Della Rodriguez. This night's work is goin' to cost you dear.'

Hallam made no reply. Instead, he turned to the men with him.

'Guess we've done what we set out to do. There can't be more'n half a dozen men left yonder.'

Mark picked out Stebbins's voice a moment later.

'You intend to let 'em go, Slim? That's plumb stupid. We got 'em all pinned down. Why not finish 'em all off. That's be six less to take care of later.'

'I think you're right, Slim,' Mark put in. 'Unless she's got friends over the border in Kenton, it won't be easy for her to bring in more hired guns.'

Hallam raised his voice. 'You men, toss your guns into

the street and then come out with your hands lifted,' he called. 'It's either that or we come in and finish you all.'

'You think we're goin' to fall for that old trick?' came the voice.

'Suit yourselves. I'm givin' you to the count o' ten. One, two, three . . .'

There was silence from Della's men.

'Four, five, six . . .'

Still the silence held. Although he could hear nothing, Mark guessed the other men were conversing among themselves in low-tones.

'Seven, eight, nine . . .'

'All right, Hallam. We're comin' out.' A second later, several guns clattered into the dusty street.

Slowly the dark figures of the gunmen moved out from the shadows of the boardwalk. All held their hands high over their heads.

'Now mount up and ride out,' Hallam said harshly. 'And don't try anythin' funny, or we'll shoot you down.'

'You're goin' to pay for this when Della hears what's happened,' snarled one of the men as he climbed into the saddle. 'It ain't finished, not by a long way. All o' you are goin' to regret you ever rode for Boardman.'

Turning their mounts, the men rode slowly out of town, leaving a slowly settling cloud of dust behind them.

Mark watched them go, then went to his own mount. After what had happened, he fell to wondering again if he had done the right thing in throwing in with Boardman and his crew. When looked at objectively, there had really been little else he could have done.

Trying to lose himself in this hell-town alone would have been impossible. Not with Ned Randers on his tail.

Since he, too, had thrown in his lot with Della, the only place of comparative safety lay with Boardman.

Della Rodriguez heard the news when the six men rode in an hour later. Not only was it unexpected, it meant that Boardman was ready to start a range war with little thought for the inevitable consequences.

The loss of these men was a bitter blow. Until now, she had been on virtually equal terms with her rival. Now, with almost a dozen good men lying in the street in town, she was at a serious disadvantage.

The anger which now always simmered just below the surface suddenly broke through as she faced the riders in the courtyard.

'Hap and Clem warned you there were plenty of Boardman's men in the saloon yet you allowed yourselves to be bushwhacked in the main street. What kind of fools have I hired to help me run this ranch and keep Boardman at bay?'

'There weren't no warnin' they meant to do anythin' like that,' protested one of the men.

'And what happened to Tollard and Cordray?' Ned Randers stepped into view beside Della, his features twisted into grim lines. 'You know anythin' of that?'

'Not much. They went into the saloon to get Dalton once we knew he'd ridden in with the others. We heard shots and those two never came out. Reckon they called out this *hombre* and he got the drop on 'em.'

Della pressed her full lips together into a hard line.

'So this man Dalton is riding with Boardman.'

'Seems so,' muttered another man.

Della stared from one man to the other, then

glanced round at Randers. Apart from the occasional burst of anger, her eyes seldom held any sign of emotion, hiding the thoughts passing through her mind. At times they would gleam with an inner fire as a reflected glint in their depths.

That glint was there now.

'I want both of you men inside. You too, Randers,' she said harshly.

Once inside she motioned the three men to the chairs around the long table before seating herself at the end.

Hap Driscoll, sitting slumped in his chair, was a small man with weasel features and a temper like a mountain lion. He had worked with Della for five years, knew her moods well. Now he could sense the fury that was smouldering inside her, ready to erupt at any moment.

Jed Norwood, on the other hand, was built like a bull, standing well over six feet tall. He gave the impression of being slow and ungainly but this was deceptive. When necessary, he could move like greased lightning.

Della settled herself more deeply into her chair. Despite her angry expression, inwardly she was worried, although she allowed none of this to show on her face. It was not her nature to show weakness in front of anyone, least of all the men who worked for her.

She glanced at Norwood.

'How many men did we lose tonight?' she asked thinly.

Norwood thought for a moment.

'Ten, twelve if you count Tollard and Cordray.'

Her expression tightened even further.

'All men I can ill afford to lose with Boardman breathing down my neck. And you can be sure he'll know about this within the hour. If he does intend to hit the Double T, he'll do it soon.'

Her sharp glance rested on Randers. Although she knew very little of him, she had the feeling he was a really cautious man. The other two were shallow men who acted without thinking. Now she had need of a man who would obey her orders to the letter and without question.

Feeling her eyes on him, Randers looked up and met her direct stare. After a moment she spoke.

'You've lost your two companions tonight and now this man Dalton knows you're the real killer of those men in Colorado. What do you intend doing? My guess is that you'll ride rather than have Dalton come looking for you.'

Randers shook his head sombrely.

'I had figured on doin' that,' he admitted drily, 'but I've changed my mind. Ain't no use runnin'. Wherever I go, Dalton will be there, knowin' what he does.'

Chewing on her lower lip, Della considered that for a moment.

'I've always got a place for a man I can trust. Maybe I can still help you get Dalton.'

'You got somethin' in mind?'

Della sat forward and placed her hands flat on the table. There was a tenseness in her which showed in every line of her body, a tautness like a coiled spring which she couldn't control.

'Boardman's got some plan in mind. Right now, I don't know what it is. But unless I get more men, he might take it into his head to wipe me out.'

'Could he do that?' Driscoll asked. 'We've still got twenty or so good men, handy with their guns. I figure he ain't got many more and—'

Della's eyes flashed dangerously.

'I didn't get to be where I am now by taking unnecessary chances.' The fingers of her right hand tapped a staccato rhythm on the table top.

'So what do you want us to do?' Norwood asked. He sat with his broad bulk on the edge of the chair as if expecting to have to get up at any moment.

'I need you and Driscoll to stay here just in case Boardman does try anything. You, Randers, I want to ride into Kenton. Hire as many gunslingers as you can. You won't be known there but they'll have heard of me. Get back here with them within the next three days, no longer. You think you can do that?'

'Kenton's over the border but I reckon I can do it. From what I've seen this country is runnin' over with gunhawks ready to sell their guns. I guess you've no objection if they're runnin' from the law.'

'None at all,' Della replied without any hesitation. 'That kind normally obey orders, especially if they're well paid.'

'When do I go?'

'First light in the morning. There's no time to waste. And it would be better if you were to stay off the trail until you're well away from Ballards Crossing. No telling who might be watching and Boardman mustn't know anything of this until I'm good and ready.'

Randers smiled viciously.

'I'll make damn sure I'm not followed.'

CHAPTER 4

AMBUSH

Hal Whitman rode along the trail to the Boardman ranch with a load of trouble on his mind. Things around Ballards Crossing were now progressing in a direction he didn't like.

There had always been bad blood between Della Rodriguez and Boardman but so far he'd been able to control it to a certain extent. Sure, their riders came into town hellbent on making noise and trouble but it had always been relatively minor incidents.

Last night, however, had been far worse than he had feared with a whole heap of Della's men killed outright in the main street. That would not go unavenged, he felt sure.

Sooner or later she would hit back and then he would have a full-scale range war on his hands. If it was limited to their own spreads, it wouldn't be too bad, they could shoot it out between themselves.

But if it started in town, the whole of Ballards

Crossing could erupt in a savage violence of gunplay right under his nose. He knew the kind of killers both ranchers had on their payrolls, men who would stop at nothing, even to wrecking the whole town.

He had known it happen in a dozen other small frontier towns and he didn't relish the thought of its happening here. He was getting too old for this job, he reflected gloomily. It needed a much younger man, one fast with a gun.

Della had already shown what she thought of him and the bitter humiliation of it had struck deep.

Even now, he wasn't sure if he was doing the right thing. The trouble was, he couldn't sit on the fence and do nothing. If he was to save his own hide and the town he had to back one or the other of these feuding ranchers. What had happened the previous morning when Della had whipped him outside his own office and turned his prisoner loose, had decided things for him.

Approaching the wide stand of trees which marked the boundary of the Circle X, he reined up sharply as a man with a Winchester stepped out of the shadows bordering the trail.

'You got any business here, Sheriff?' Stebbins asked harshly. 'If not, you can turn around and head back into town.'

'I want a word with Clem Boardman,' Whitman said, swallowing hard. 'It's important and I'm sure he'll want to hear what I have to tell him.'

A pause, then: 'All right. Go on through.'

Sitting taut in the saddle, Whitman pushed his mount forward. When he had gone fifty yards, he turned to glance over his shoulder. There was no sign of the man. Evidently, he thought, Boardman was taking no chances of any of Della's men getting through.

There were several men in the courtyard when he rode up. He noticed Mark instantly, standing near the barn. He signalled him over.

'You all right, Mark?' he asked in a low tone, aware that some of the men were watching closely.

Mark gave a quick nod. 'Sure, I'm fine. What brings you here? Somethin' to do with last night?'

'Afraid so. But I'll have to talk with Clem Boardman about that.' He broke off, dismounted and went towards the house, pausing on the veranda as the door opened and Boardman came out.

'I hope you ain't come to complain about that little fracas last night, Sheriff.' Boardman spoke around the thick cigar between his lips. If he was surprised to see the sheriff there, he gave no sign as he motioned Whitman inside and closed the door. 'Those men had it comin' to them for killin' four of mine. If Della wants to start somethin', then I aim to finish it.'

Before Whitman could reply Boardman stepped forward and peered more closely at the sheriff, noticing the ugly weals down the sides of the lawman's face.

'You don't need to tell me how you got those,' he said. 'Della Rodriguez. I can recognize the marks of her whip anywhere. You sure must've got on the wrong side of her.'

'That ain't why I'm here, leastways not directly.'

'Then why have you come?'

'Della lost quite a few of her men last night when your boys bushwhacked them in town.'

'You think I'm goin' to shed any tears over that?' Boardman uttered a derisive laugh.

'Nope. But there's something I figure you'd like to know. I overheard talk in the saloon an hour or so ago. Seems she's wastin' no time gettin' more men. She's sendin' some *hombre* called Randers to Kenton to bring back another bunch. My guess is he'll be back with 'em in two or three days.'

Boardman's eyes narrowed down a shade. For a couple of minutes he stood quite still, staring in front of him. Then he stirred himself, realized that his cigar had gone out and relit it, blowing smoke into the air.

'Just why are you tellin' me this, Whitman?' he asked suspiciously. 'We ain't exactly seen eye to eye on a lot o' things. You must have a reason.'

Whitman ran his tongue over lips that had suddenly gone dry. He forced himself to hold the other's piercing stare. At last he spoke.

'If Della gets these men, she'll hit you – and hit you hard. I was elected to uphold the law in Ballards Crossing but there ain't no way I can do that with the two of you at each other's throats.'

'So you figure that if one of us finishes the other for good, things might settle down.'

Whitman nodded.

'But why me?' Suspicion and doubt still edged Boardman's tone.

Whitman put up a hand to his face and gingerly ran his fingers along the marks there.

'I reckon you can see why for yourself,' he replied flatly.

Boardman's lips drew back in a faint smile.

'I suppose we do both have a reason for wantin' to drive her out.' He moved to the door. 'Thanks for this information, Sheriff. You may be sure I intend to act on it.'

He waited until the lawman had vanished round the bend in the trail and then called Stebbins and Hallam. He pointed to Mark.

'I want you in on this too, Dalton,' he said.

Mark waited while the others had gone into the house before following, closing the door quietly behind him. The thought occurred to him that Boardman had somehow figured out he was in some way connected with the sheriff. If that were so, he could find himself in a tight spot.

'I've just been given some interestin' news by the sheriff,' Boardman said without preamble. 'Seems Della is sendin' this stranger, Randers, into Kenton to bring in more gunhawks.'

'Randers!' Mark glanced up in surprise. 'Why would she send him instead of one of her own men? He's nothin' more than a two-bit killer.'

Boardman scratched the stubble on his chin.

'Guess you know more about him than we do. You suppose he might just cut and run after you killed his partners?'

'There's a chance, I reckon. But my opinion is that he's relyin' on Della to protect him until he can get me. He knows I've got him dead to rights about the murder I was accused of.'

Boardman gave a nod. His eyes were darkly shadowed in speculative thought.

'One thing's for sure,' he said soberly. 'We have to

stop those men reachin' Della's spread. There's no doubt that if Randers does carry out her orders, he'll easily pick up a score o' men willin' to do anythin' for her, from rustlin' our beef to killin' off my men. I can't allow that.'

'You want some of us to ride out and keep an eye on that trail, boss?' Hallam asked. 'I know of one place where we can jump 'em before they get here.'

Boardman thought that over, deliberating, but only for a few seconds. Then he nodded.

'Take half a dozen of the boys with you, Slim,' he said ominously. 'You go with 'em too, Dalton. You know this *hombre* Randers better than most.'

Half a day after Randers left the Rodriguez spread Mark rode out with the Circle X men. They rode north-east with Hallam and Stebbins in the lead, showing the way. It was well over a day's ride to Kenton but they didn't intend going all that way.

A while along the trail, they cut off, moving towards the edge of the Badlands, a vast wilderness of parched soil where nothing grew but the clumps of bitter sage.

Slim and Chet rode side by side, a short distance in front of Mark and the others. Conversation was virtually non-existent. Each man was engrossed in his own thoughts. All were seasoned gunfighters but even so, the odds might be stacked against them if Randers succeeded in bringing a large number of men with him.

Mark rode low in the saddle, his hat-brim pulled down to just above his eyes, providing only a little shade from the stabbing glare of the sun. He had known country like this back in Colorado, knew they were in for a long, hard ride where there was no cover from the brilliant sunlight.

Here and there large masses of tumbleweed careered over the flat, monotonous landscape, blown by the hot wind from the south-west. Great balls of dried vegetation, they were the only things that moved in the eye-searing heat.

'You figured out the best place to ambush these gunhawks, Slim?' called one of the men.

'There's a narrow pass about fifteen miles ahead called Devil's Rock,' Hallam answered without turning his head. 'If we can get 'em hemmed in there, we'll have the advantage of surprise and a good position.'

'Fifteen miles in this blisterin' heat,' grumbled another man.

'That's right. You got any complaints you can give 'em to Boardman when we get back.'

After that there was no more grumbling, the men riding on in a sullen silence. The sun was a blazing furnace in a cloudless sky and there was very little wind to mitigate the intense heat that poured down on them like the inside of an oven.

The afternoon passed with a nightmare slowness, the sun edging past its zenith, their shadows short beside them. Peering through red-rimmed eyes, Mark could see why they had to travel so far from Ballards Crossing to ambush any men riding in from Kenton.

Here the terrain was almost completely flat, there was no cover for man or beast. Any men approaching from the north could spot them for miles.

Shortly before sundown a curious, irregularly shaped mass showed on the horizon. It stood out clearly against the heavens in that direction. Very soon he realized that the trail Hallam and Stebbins were following would lead them directly to it.

As if confirming his thoughts, Hap abruptly pulled his mount to a standstill and pointed.

'There's the place,' he said hoarsely. 'We should reach it just after nightfall. Once there, we wait.'

'That where you intend to hit 'em?' asked one of the men riding beside Mark.

'It's the only place this side o' the border,' Hallam explained.

'And the one place where they'll be doubly cautious,' Mark pointed out.

'That's true. But don't worry, we'll all be well hidden.'

'You know somethin' of this *hombre* Randers?' Chet put in. 'You reckon he's the cautious type?'

'All I really know of him is that he's a two-bit killer, probably wanted for murder in half a dozen states. Some reckon he's as fast as lightnin' with a gun but my opinion is that most of the men he's killed, he's shot in the back like my two friends.'

Anxious to get out of the heat and the glare reflected off the ground by the slowly setting sun, the men urged their mounts forward at as fast a pace as they dared. Straining his vision through the shimmering air, Mark tried to make out details of the long black shape ahead of them.

It looked like a hog's back rising about 200 feet from the flatness of its surroundings. But it was more than a simple promontory lifting from the Badlands.

Not until an hour had passed did any real detail

emerge. Then, gradually, he recognized that it was truly a massive rock formation, the narrow trail cutting right through the centre of it.

What had made it appear so curious were the tall spires of rock which towered on either side: great columns of jagged stone, now black with shadow. It looked the ideal place for an ambush, too ideal.

Mark recognized at once that if Randers did ride back this way with a bunch of men, they might also realize this and be doubly cautious. By the time they rode between the gaunt, rising walls of stone, it was almost dark. The last colours of sunset were fading swiftly towards the west and already the temperature was dropping.

They dismounted well inside the ravine, not bothering to tether their mounts, knowing they were just as weary as themselves and unlikely to stray far. Here and there among the rocks stunted sage bushes grew out of the sparse soil.

'Two o' you men collect some of that sage and start a fire,' Hap ordered.

'Is that wise?' Mark muttered.

'There ain't no chance of anyone bein' within twenty miles of here,' Slim maintained. 'And I doubt if Randers has reached Kenton yet.'

Most of the sage was dried and withered and the men had soon gathered enough to make a fire. The aromatic smell of the smoke caught at their throats as it lifted high into the heavens.

Squatting around the fire, they ate a cold meal but one washed down with hot coffee brewed over the leaping flames.

Mark glanced up. 'Where do you think we should lay

this ambush, Slim?' he asked, tautly.

Hallam pointed. 'There's a fairly wide ledge running along both sides o' the canyon. We move up there. Those stone columns will provide us with plenty o' cover.'

Mark nodded. 'I been thinkin'. There's somethin' else we can do.'

A gust of enquiry swept across Hallam's face.

'What's that?'

'Even if we take down a goodly number o' these gunslingers, the rest will try to make a run for it and with our mounts up there among the rocks, those who did would have a good start. We'd never catch up with them before they hit the Double T.'

'So what do you suggest?' Chet put in.

'Gather up as much o' that sage as we can and block that exit with it and some o' those tumbleweeds. Once the shootin' starts, one of us puts a torch to it. I don't reckon many o' their mounts will want to pass that.'

'Good thinkin'.' Chet nodded. He threw a quick glance at the sky. 'Guess we'd better get some sleep while we can.'

'Don't we post a look-out?' Mark asked.

Hallam shook his head. 'Like I said, Randers won't be headin' back this way much before tomorrow night.'

'I wasn't thinkin' of him,' Mark replied. 'But it could be that Della suspects we know somethin' of her little plan. She could've sent some of her men after us, hoping to catch us off guard.'

Hallam pursed his lips into a hard line, brows drawn down over his eyes. Then he got to his feet, staring back along the canyon into the darkness lying beyond the rim of the firelight.

'Hadn't considered that,' he admitted. 'Ain't likely unless she's been keepin' an eye on the sheriff.' He glanced down at one of the men near the fire. 'You take the first two hours, Seth, then you take over, Slim. Mark, you can take the last watch.'

Mark nodded and moved a little way from the fire. He rolled himself into his blanket. Lying there, staring up into the star-flecked heavens, he wondered what Janet Casson and her father would think if they knew what he was doing. He guessed they had no liking for Della or Boardman, that as far as they were concerned both were tarred with the same brush.

He heard Seth move softly away to keep watch at the end of the ravine. Then he was asleep, surrendering himself to the deep weariness that overwhelmed him.

Someone shaking him by the shoulder brought him out of the deep sleep. He sat up and found Chet bending over him. Instantly awake, he thrust himself to his feet, buckled on his gunbelt, and made it to the end of the canyon.

The fact that he had not been wakened earlier clearly indicated there had been no incidents so far. He settled himself with his shoulders against a rocky spur and built a smoke, striking the sulphur match on the rock. By now his eyes had grown accustomed to the darkness and in the faint moonlight he could see for quite a distance.

There was a deep stillness all around him. Only the faint snicker of a horse disturbed the silence. More than once he pondered the possibility that Randers had taken this chance to ride out of the territory, to keep riding in the hope that he would not be trailed and brought back to face justice at the end of a rope.

He knew very little of what kind of woman Della Rodriguez was. Hard, callous and ruthless, certainly. A woman who knew exactly what she wanted and would do anything to achieve her ambitions. Nothing was to stand in the way of her becoming the biggest name in the entire territory. Such women could be extremely dangerous and he knew that, if cornered, she would fight like a wildcat with everything at her disposal.

But was she the kind who owed any loyalty to the men who worked for her? Somehow he thought not. Once Randers' usefulness was finished, he felt sure she would throw him to the dogs, particularly if his presence should pose any threat to her plans.

If such a though ever entered Randers's head, he would cut and run, desperate to save his own life. Perhaps he had done that and they had ridden all this way for nothing.

He sat there, absorbed in these thoughts, until the dawn brightened and the rest of the men began to stir. Following another cold meal, the men gathered all of the dry sage and some of the gigantic tumbleweeds, stacking them tightly across the end of the canyon.

Very soon they had succeeded in building a barrier some ten feet high, blocking the exit completely. Slim nodded his satisfaction.

'Once we fire that they'll be trapped inside,' he muttered. 'I doubt if their mounts will try to break through.'

He glanced around for comment, shrugged when there was none. 'Now all we have to do is position ourselves and wait. Four men on either side. My guess is that Randers won't waste any time in Kenton. That town is full o' gunhawks ready and willin' to ride for anybody who pays well. And I guess Della Rodriguez is as well-known there as she is in Ballards Crossing.'

'So you figure he should be approachin' here in around twelve hours,' Mark said.

'That's my guess. Once he gets the men he wants, ain't no cause for him to stay any longer than necessary.' Slim threw an appraising glance at the massive walls of rock that enclosed the trail. 'There are a couple of narrow tracks leadin' up yonder on both sides. We split into two groups, take our mounts up there and spread out along the whole length o' the ravine.'

'And the barrier at the end?' Chet put in. 'That's goin' to be a mite tricky. Ain't no sense settin' it afire before they're all inside the canyon.'

'I've thought about that. One of us waits among those rocks at the end. Once the firin' starts, that'll be the signal to put a light to it. Shouldn't be too difficult with a brand.'

'I'll do that,' said Mark evenly.

Slim's shrewd glance rested on him for a moment. There seemed to be other thoughts running through his mind. Then he nodded in acquiescence.

'All right. Just make sure you do it right when the time comes. I don't want any o' those men to get out o' this alive.'

Mark spoke through tightly-clenched teeth.

'I want Randers alive if possible. He's mine.'

Hap shrugged. 'If you can take him alive, he's yours. Guess I can understand your reasons.'

*

The day dragged by in a haze of heat. Even in the shadow thrown by the high wall of rock the air brought the sweat out of every pore. Each man was now in his place, completely hidden from the view of anyone below.

It had been a difficult task, getting their mounts up what were little more than animal tracks to the broader ledges some fifty feet above the canyon floor. Now every man lay and sweated, waiting for the evening. Only Mark and Slim remained at the bottom of the ravine.

They were standing at the far end of the canyon. The tightly packed sage and tumbleweed were as dry as tinder. It would need only the touch of a lighted brand to set fire to it across its whole length.

Mark eyed the mass of tumbled boulders with a critical gaze. As Slim had said, there were plenty of places there to provide him with cover. But he would have to choose a spot with care. If those riders attempted to rush the barrier he wanted to be well away from the stampeding horses.

'You sure you want to go through with this?' Slim asked, breaking the uncomfortable silence. 'I can always get one o' the others.'

Mark shook his head.

'Nope. I'll do it.' He knew everything could depend upon split-second timing.

When they came those riders would be pushing their mounts to the limit. He estimated the ravine to be about half a mile in length, possibly a little longer.

A lot was going to depend upon two things: whether

Randers would approach with some degree of caution, in case Boardman knew of this – and what those gunhawks would do once the shooting started.

Would they spur their mounts to get out of gunshot range as quickly as possible, or would they make a dive for cover, intending to fight it out?

In either case he judged he would have less than a minute to fire the barrier and get under cover.

CHAPTER 5

DEATH OUT OF
THE NIGHT

The evening was just deepening into dusk but there was still enough light to make out the white dust-cloud in the distance. Mark scanned it.

'I reckon there must be at least twenty riders in that bunch,' he said softly. 'Seems Randers has done a lot o' talkin' in Kenton to get all those men to back Della.'

'I never figured he'd bring in as many as that.' Slim breathed the words in a long exhalation. 'Could be we'll have a real fight on our hands.'

'Leastways we've got the advantage of surprise on our side.'

'Then we'd better make the most of it.' Slim turned and called up to the men concealed behind the rising pillars of stone. 'They're comin' now. Wait until they're all inside the canyon before you open fire, and make every shot count.'

Leaving Mark, he scrambled up the narrow track and a moment later had disappeared from view. Mark hesitated for a moment, then ran for the end of the canyon, heading into the rough cluster of rocks to one side.

Half-way along its length the canyon bent to the left. Those men riding in would see nothing of the barrier until they were at least half-way through it. Even then, it would be difficult to make out details in the rapidly darkening night.

Resting his shoulders against the rock, he held the brand in his left hand, ready to be lit once the signal was given. This was going to be the tricky bit. With the flaring brand in his hand, he would make a perfect target for any of those gunmen.

Now he could just make out the steady drumming of hoofbeats in the distance and knew the riders were swiftly approaching the far end of the canyon. His own mount was tethered to some brush a short distance away around the edge of the escarpment and he knew it would make no sound to betray his presence.

The sound of horses came closer and to his keen hearing they seemed to be slowing a little, as if Randers was wary of approaching the narrow cutting. He waited, tension in every fibre of his body.

After a few minutes he felt certain that all of the riders must be well inside the canyon, that at any moment there might come a yell to indicate that one of them had spotted the barrier. Still the silence dragged itself out with an agonizing slowness.

Then, with a startling abruptness that made him flinch, the roar of gunfire echoed and re-echoed along

the ravine. The sound was magnified by the reverbera-
tions rebounding from the stone walls. Swiftly, he struck
the match, applied it to the rags at the end of the long
branch. It flared into flame immediately.

Getting his feet under him, he darted forward,
thrusting the blazing torch against the brush. He waited
tensely until the flames caught.

Head low, bent almost double, he moved swiftly
across the entire width of the canyon, pushing in the
brand at four places before running back.

The fiery touch of the flames caught at his exposed
face and hands. There came several harsh shouts. The
next moment lead rattled through the blazing sage.
More slugs hummed over his head, whining off the
nearby rocks.

Desperately he threw himself into the shelter of the
boulders. His shoulder struck an outjutting spur of
stone sending a lance of agony searing along his arm.
Then he was crouched behind a massive boulder. A
couple of slugs ricocheted off the stone as he pulled the
Colts from their holsters.

Deeper within the canyon confusion reigned among
the riders as bullets came at them from either side. A
number of them toppled from the saddle within
seconds. The others milled around, struggling to
control their rearing mounts and get a sight on their
attackers. But the Circle X men were well-concealed
high above them.

Even from where he crouched among the rocks
Mark distinctly heard Randers's voice raised above the
others.

'This is Boardman's doin'. Someone must've warned

him. We've got to get out of here or we're all finished.'

Mark's eyes narrowed as he risked a quick glance around the side of the boulder. In the darkness, it was impossible to make out many details. The stabbing lances of gunfire speared in all directions. Shadowy figures were just visible, aiming wildly into the higher reaches. Men yelled thinly as lead tore into them.

Aiming swiftly at a dark shape racing his mount straight for the blazing obstruction, he squeezed the trigger, saw the man throw up his arms and fall. The riderless horse continued to run forward, crashing into the barrier, sending sparks flying in all directions.

The next moment several of the gunmen still in the saddle raced their mounts towards the narrow gap. Through smoke-grimed eyes, Mark recognized Randers in the lead. Swinging his Colt, he loosed off another couple of shots, swore under his breath as both missed.

Then Randers was through, raking spurs along the horse's flanks in his frantic haste to get away. Mark caught a glimpse of the other's face stretched into a rictus of terror. Instinctively, he sent another shot after him, but within seconds Randers was a rapidly disappearing shadow as he put his mount to the trail.

Attempting to follow him, two riders crashed into each other. One succeeded in getting through the narrow gap in the flames. The other failed to control his mount as it stumbled on the uneven surface. Pitching from the saddle, the gunman fell in front of the pounding hoofs of the oncoming riders.

Behind the fleeing men the gunfire gradually lessened. Mark levered himself cautiously upright and leaned against the rock for a few moments, coughing on the smoke going down into his lungs. The scorching heat of the flames still seared his face as he slowly eased him way down on to the canyon floor.

He thrusted fresh shells into the Colts and went forward, straining his vision to pick out the figures lying sprawled against the rocks. A couple of the men were still alive.

Seeing him approaching, one attempted to lift his gun and line it up on him. But there was no strength left in the man's body. The Colt tilted in his nerveless fingers and dropped into the dust beside him as his head went back and he lay still. The other had a smashed shoulder and a bullet in his leg.

Keeping him covered, Mark glanced up swiftly as Slim approached. There was a grim smile just visible on the foreman's features.

'Reckon we got most of 'em,' he said thickly. 'Did you get any back there?' He inclined his head towards the canyon exit.

'One. But I figure that about half a dozen managed to break through. Randers was among 'em.'

'Guess he'll keep until another day.'

'Unless Della decides to make an example of him.' Chet had overheard. He came forward and stared down at the bodies strewn all around them. 'She don't take too kindly to men who make mistakes. I sure wouldn't like to be in his boots when he has to explain this to her.'

'You think she might run him out o' town?' Mark asked. He knew that if that happened he might never get a chance to bring Randers in.

'Could be. She ain't known for her good temper. Or

she'll see to it that he's shot. It'll be made to look like an accident or that Boardman killed him.'

'Damn.' Mark swore softly between his teeth.

'You may still get your chance,' Slim said tautly. 'I reckon that so long as Randers can use a gun Della will see to it that he stays. Even with those men who got away, I doubt if she's in a position to attack the Circle X spread unless she figures there's no other choice.'

They called the rest of the men together and rode out of the canyon with the wounded man over the back of one of the horses. Half an hour later the moon rose, flooding the plain with yellow.

Now they deliberately avoided the trail, knowing there was the distinct possibility that those men who had escaped their ambush might be lying in wait for them. In the moonlight it was possible to see for several miles in every direction. There were long shadows but nothing moved apart from the ever-present tumble-weeds rolling along their endless tracks across the mesa.

The moon traced its yellow course across the heavens, setting just before the grey dawn brightened towards the east. All the way they saw no sign of Randers and the others. By now, Mark mused, they would have reached the Double T ranch.

Whether Randers would tell the truth as to how many men he had been able to recruit in Kenton, or would tell the few with him to say they were the only ones, he didn't know. Either way, he had the idea that Della would be far from pleased.

'You did a mighty fine job tonight, boys,' Boardman

said genially. 'You say this bounty hunter, Randers, had at least twenty men with him when they were headed this way?'

'Possibly a few more,' Stebbins said. 'They rode straight into the ambush without thinkin' it might be a trap. Dalton here came up with the smart idea o' blockin' the exit with dry sage and once he fired that, they ran into big trouble.'

Boardman rubbed a hand down the side of his face, his forehead furrowed in thought.

'Six of 'em managed to get away, you say?' He puffed hard on his cigar and blew the smoke out in twin streams through his nostrils. After a reflective pause, he went on: 'It could still spell trouble for us. Right now, that's somethin' I don't want.'

'You think that even with just six more Della might push her luck and either rustle your beef or strike here?'

'It's possible. There's no way o' tellin' what that woman has in mind.' He walked over to the window and stood staring out into the brightening daylight. 'Just to be on the safe side, I want the riders out with the herd doubled.'

'That would leave us a bit stretched here if she decides to attack the ranch house instead,' Hallam muttered.

'I'm well aware of that. But it's a risk I'll have to take. With only an additional six men compared with the twenty or so she was hopin' for, it ain't likely she'll try to hit us here.'

'What do we do with the *hombre* we brought in?' Slim enquired. 'He's pretty badly shot up.'

'We'll have to get the doc for him. Maybe he'll decide to work for me. His type owe allegiance to nobody unless they're paid. If not, we'll turn him loose. It's unlikely he'll go over to Della's side after what happened.'

At the Double T ranch Della Rodriguez had waited impatiently for over an hour for Randers to return. When she saw him ride in with only six men at his back, her face twisted into a scowl of fury.

'Are these all the men you managed to get?' she demanded, her voice thin with anger and disappointment.

Randers felt a little shiver run along his spine at her tone and the expression on her face. All the way back he had been debating inwardly what to tell her. For a moment he considered lying, then rejected the idea instantly.

If she should find out from anyone else what had happened, that lie would certainly mean the end of him. He had faced up to several men with the mean streak of a desert wolf in them, but this woman was different.

'Somebody must've talked,' he said harshly, somehow getting the words out. 'Boardman's men were waitin' for us at Devil Rock and—'

'How many men did you hire in Kenton?' Her words were like the lash of her whip.

'Twenty-two.'

'You hired twenty-two men for me, all reputedly fast with a gun, and I'll wager there were less than half that number of Boardman's crew.'

80

Randers flinched at the naked scorn in her tone. For a moment her hand dropped towards the whip in her belt. Then she withdrew it slowly, leaving the whip where it was.

Randers let out a long exhalation.

'There ain't no blame on me,' he said, 'or the men with me. You know that place. Half a dozen men could cut down an army without exposin' themselves to any return fire. Not only that but they'd blocked the exit with sage and fired it.'

Della made to utter another sharp retort, then thought better of it. Still fuming, she said harshly:

'You're sure someone talked?'

'How else could they know to be lyin' in wait? It was a well-prepared trap. They must've been there more than a day settin' it up.'

Della's dark brows drew together, her lips pressed into a hard line. Looking at Randers, she said with a deceptive softness:

'Only four of us knew you were riding into Kenton for these men. I told no one and I don't think you would jeopardize your life by talking.'

A faint smile passed over Randers' features. So it had to be either Jed Norwood or Hap Driscoll. Now that the guilt had been transferred from him to the other two men, he felt a little easier in his mind.

'If it was either of them who talked carelessly I'll certainly get it out of them.' The way she said it froze the blood in Randers's veins. He had considered her to be hard when she had confronted the sheriff but apart from that one incident, this was a side of her he had not previously encountered. He could really believe some

81

of the stories he had heard: that Della Rodriguez was the Devil incarnate.

She drew herself up to her full height.

'You men get something to eat and rest up,' she said thinly. 'I have a job for you and some of the others later.'

Randers glanced up sharply.

'You intend to hit Boardman?' He knew as soon as he spoke that he shouldn't question her in this way but she seemed to take no offence.

Smiling, she nodded.

'He'll be expecting us to hit his herd, or perhaps go up against the ranch house.'

'But that ain't what you got in mind.'

'No. While he has all his men either watching the herd or around the house I mean to hit him where he'll be least expecting it and where it'll be equally bad for him.'

There was a puzzled look on Randers's angular features which she noticed at once. For a moment, her vicious smile widened.

'Where do you think I lost most of my men? Not here or on the range.'

Randers jerked his head up in sudden understanding.

'You're goin' to hit his saloons in town.'

'That's my plan. My guess is there'll be scarcely any of his men there tonight. He'll need them all at the Circle X. By the time I'm finished, all that will be left of those saloons will be heaps of smoking ruin.' She uttered a short laugh but there was no mirth in it and the sound made Randers cringe.

As he turned to leave, she added thinly: 'And not a word of this to Norwood or Driscoll. If I have a low-down snake among my crew, I intend to stamp on him.'

Della was seated behind the large mahogany desk when Driscoll and Norwood entered. Both men seemed surprised to have received this summons.

'You wanted to see us, Miss Della?' Driscoll said, focusing on her face, trying to read something there.

Della looked up from the papers which lay in front of her.

'That's right. I suppose you both know that Randers ran into trouble, big trouble, last night on his way back with the men he hired for me in Kenton.'

For a moment, neither man said anything. Then Norwood spoke, with a trace of nervousness in his tone.

'We did see him ride in with some men a little while ago.'

'There were more than twenty men when they set out from Kenton. But Boardman's crew were waiting for them at Devil Rock. The rest of those men are lying back there in the canyon, possibly with the vultures already picking them clean.'

Norwood threw an oblique glance at his companion, consternation written all over his face.

'But what's that got to do with us?'

Thrusting her chair back with a sharp movement, Della got to her feet.

'I'll tell you what it has to do with you,' she stormed. 'Apart from Randers and myself, only the two of you knew he was heading for Kenton to hire more gunmen after I lost all those men in town.

'Both of you were in Ballards Crossing a couple of days ago. If neither of you went straight to Boardman with that information, then someone in town got it from you.'

'But I never said a word to anyone,' Driscoll protested.

'Neither did I,' Norwood put in. 'If you're sayin' that we deliberately—'

Della's lips thinned down into an ugly grimace.

'I'm saying that whether you did it deliberately, or made careless talk and someone overheard, you're both fired. I won't have men on my payroll I can't trust implicitly. I want both of you off my land within the hour. Got that?'

Driscoll made to protest, then clamped his lips tightly together, knowing it would be useless to argue with her.

'Now get out of my sight, both of you. And if you're anywhere in this territory by noon, I'll send some of the boys after you.'

Twenty minutes later both men climbed into the saddle and rode out of the Double T.

From the door of the bunkhouse Ned Randers watched them go with an expression of satisfaction on his saturnine features. He had guessed what had happened in Della's room when she had confronted the two men, although he doubted if either man had passed on that information to Boardman.

Almost certainly they had merely spoken of it between themselves in the Golden Horseshoe and someone had overheard. But however it had happened, he intended to turn it to his own advantage. With

Driscoll gone as the Double T foreman, if he played his cards right there was the possibility he might get that job for himself.

He was sure that Della believed he had had no part in it, putting his own life on the line. Perhaps she still blamed him for not taking the precaution of thinking ahead and foreseeing there might be an ambush at Devil Rock but that was something he felt sure he could overcome.

As Hap Driscoll sat taut in the saddle his mind seethed with a turbulence of angry thoughts. His fingers on the reins clenched tightly with savage fury.

For several years he had served Della Rodriguez faithfully, carrying out every order without question. Now, without warning, he and his companion had been dismissed without any chance to defend themselves against her accusations.

Perhaps it had entered into some conversation he'd had with Norwood in the saloon but as far as he had been aware there had been no one close enough to hear anything of what they were saying.

For a moment his anger was turned away from Della to Randers. They knew nothing of this man who had suddenly appeared in Ballards Crossing, claiming to be a bounty hunter on the trail of some killer.

Maybe he was the one who had talked. Maybe he was in the pay of Boardman and had passed on the news to the other. He turned that possibility over in his mind but eventually rejected it.

From what little he had heard, Randers had been lucky to escape with his life. If he had known those men were lying in wait for him, it was unlikely he would have deliberately ridden into that ambush, knowing it was just as likely he would collect a slug as any of those riding with him.

Norwood broke the uncomfortable silence between them. 'What do you intend doin' now, Hap?' he grated. 'Ride on for some other spread?'

Driscoll did not speak for several moments, then he rasped:

'Nope. I mean to get even with Della for what she's just done. No one does this to me and gets away with it, not even Della.'

Norwood turned to look directly at him.

'You ain't thinkin' of ridin' back there and startin' trouble, are you? Della would have you shot the minute you rode in.'

'I ain't such a fool as that,' Driscoll retorted. 'But I know somethin' that Della doesn't want to get out.'

'What's that?'

'Just before pullin' out I went back into the bunkhouse for my gunbelt. Randers was there with a few of the boys. They didn't see me and they was talkin' in low voices but I overheard enough to know that Della means to hit Boardman's saloons tonight.'

'You ain't thinkin' of telling this to Boardman?'

'Can you think of any better way of gettin' back at Della?'

Norwood pondered that, then shook his head. 'I want no part o' that,' he replied. 'If Della should find out your life won't be worth a plugged nickel. She'd hunt you down if it was the last thing she did.'

He reined his mount and indicated the rough trail

that led northward. 'I'm ridin' out while I'm still alive. You do what you think best.'

Driscoll watched him go, remaining there until the other disappeared round a sharp bend in the trail. Then, with a jerk on the bridle, he wheeled his mount and headed for the boundary which separated the Double T from Boardman's range.

He had ridden for barely a mile when he came upon the herd and here, two of the rimriders swung away, their Winchesters levelled at him.

'Just hold it right there,' called one of the men. He paused as recognition came. 'What the hell are you doin' here, Driscoll?'

'Driscoll,' muttered the second man. 'Ain't he Della's foreman?' His expression hardened. 'Better shuck that gunbelt, friend.'

'You're trespassing on Boardman's land,' put in the other. 'He won't care overmuch if we take you in, dead or alive.'

Very slowly, Driscoll unbuckled the gunbelt and let it fall to the ground. While the second man kept him covered, the other dismounted and removed the Winchester from Driscoll's scabbard.

'I've got some information for Boardman,' Driscoll said. 'I reckon it's something he'll want to hear.'

'All right.' The first man picked up the gunbelt. 'Clint here will take you to him. Then it's up to the boss to decide what to do with you. If this is one o' Della's tricks, you'll regret ever comin' here.'

Keeping his hands in sight, Driscoll rode on with the rimrider just a little way behind him, his rifle pointed directly at Hap's back.

They came within sight of the ranch house half an hour later, when Clint motioned Driscoll to step down. He herded him to the veranda and knocked loudly on the door.

Boardman appeared a few moments later. His hard gaze flicked intently over Driscoll.

'Where did you find him, Clint?' he asked.

'Ridin' the west pasture, Mr Boardman. Reckons he's got some information for you.'

'That so?' Boardman eyed Driscoll with a speculative look in his eyes. 'And just what is this information?'

Driscoll ran his tongue over dry lips.

'Della is plannin' to hit you tonight.'

Boardman's lips twisted slightly into a mirthless grin. 'I'd already guessed she might once those killers joined her.'

'Mebbe so, but you don't know where she means to strike.'

Boardman stepped forward until he was only a couple of inches from the other. His eyes bored into Driscoll's.

'When Della's foreman comes ridin' in with information like this, I get a bad feelin' in my guts. If she figured she can trick me into movin' my men around to suit her, she's goddamn mistaken.'

'Better hear him out.' Mark was standing a few feet away and had heard what Driscoll had said. 'We can soon find out if he's lyin' or not.'

For a moment a spark of fury blazed in the rancher's eyes, then he forced himself to calm down.

'Speak your piece and then ride back to Della and tell her she ain't foolin' me.'

Driscoll swallowed hard.

'I ain't the foreman of the Double T any more,' he said thinly. 'Those men she was bringin' in from Kenton got hit last night. More than half of 'em was killed at Devil Rock but I guess you know all about that.'

Boardman nodded. 'Go on,' he grated.

'Della reckons it was me and Norwood who told you about those men. She fired us both, gave us until noon to quit the territory or she'd send her gunmen after us.'

Boardman digested that for a short while, running it over in his mind. Then he said sharply:

'So instead of ridin' out, you decided to come to see me, hopin' I'd believe you and take you on.'

'I worked for years carryin' out her orders. It don't sit well with me to be treated like this. I aim to get back at her. If you ain't interested in what I've got to say, then I guess I'll have to get my revenge in some other way.'

He made as if to turn, then stopped as Boardman snapped sharply:

'All right, Driscoll. Speak your piece.'

'Just before I rode out I overheard this *hombre* Randers tellin' some of the boys to get ready for a job tonight. She's guessed you'd expect her to hit your herd or make a strike against this place. Instead, she means to wreck your saloons in town.'

Boardman's eyes widened slightly. It was the only change of expression he made. Swinging, he glanced at Mark where he stood with Hallam and Stebbins.

'What do you reckon?' he demanded.

Clem shrugged. 'Guess he could be tellin' the truth. It's the devious sort o' thing Della would do.'

'Trouble is, we've got no easy way of tellin' whether

he's lyin or not. If he is, it could be a ruse to draw men away from her.' Boardman scratched his ear.

'There's one way we could cover ourselves,' Mark said.

'How's that?'

'I could ride into town with one of your boys. We got two things in our favour. I doubt if Della will consider the possibility of Driscoll or Norwood comin' here with this information. She's bankin' on everyone being here or with the herd so she won't send many men into town.'

Boardman was dubious.

'Then you reckon just two o' you could handle it?'

'I guess so.' Mark forced confidence into his voice. 'Just so long as you keep this *hombre* here where he can't talk.'

'Don't worry none about that,' Boardman replied grimly. 'He ain't goin' nowhere.'

CHAPTER 6

BAPTISM BY FIRE

It was early evening when Mark and Chet rode into Ballards Crossing. The town seemed unnaturally quiet even for that hour. In the street, the day's heat was beginning to dissipate a little but it was still too hot for comfort.

As Mark tethered his mount a voice he recognized hailed him from the other side of the main street.

Turning, he noticed the small buckboard which stood in front of the small store. Janet Casson sat there, waving across to him.

'A friend o' yours?' Chet asked as he dismounted.

'They were good enough to give me food and a bed when I first rode into this territory with three bounty hunters on my tail.'

As he went over, Sam Casson came out of the store, carrying a couple of large sacks which he tossed into the back of the wagon. He was limping badly and it was clear his leg was still giving him a lot of pain.

'I see you're still here, Mark,' Janet said. She threw a quick look towards Chet, then looked back to him. 'We thought you'd maybe ridden out or been killed by those bounty hunters who were after you.'

Mark shook his head.

'Two of them are dead, but the third joined up with Della Rodriguez. One thing I did learn. The man, Randers, is the one who killed my friends. Then he and the others framed me for the murder.'

'Then if he's workin' for her, how come you're still alive?' Sam enquired. 'She ain't the kind o' woman to fool around with. I'd have thought she'd have sent her men after you.'

'So I've discovered. Sheriff Whitman helped me as much as he could but there ain't much he can do with her tryin' to run this territory. I got a job with Boardman.'

'Clem Boardman?' There was genuine surprise in the old man's tone and something else which Mark couldn't quite figure out. 'There are some who reckon he's just as bad as Della.'

'So I've heard. And that's what I first thought him to be.'

Janet's brow furrowed a little.

'So what made you change your mind about him?'

'Hard to say. So far I ain't seen or heard anythin' to suggest that he's tried to run anyone off their spreads and he's been here in Ballards Crossing a lot longer than Della. My guess is he's strugglin' to keep his land and cattle, but if Della has her way she'll run him off no matter what it takes.'

'Could be you're right.' Sam didn't sound

convinced. 'He's got the biggest herd o' beef around, so I guess he's a lot more to lose if she gets her way. If Della does make a move like that, it'll spark off a full-scale range war and I wouldn't want to be in the middle o' that.'

'You headin' back to the ranch now?'

'Sure. Just came in for some supplies.' Sam jerked a thumb towards the sacks in the back as he climbed awkwardly up beside Janet. 'Why'd you ask?'

'There might be trouble in town pretty soon.'

'What sort of trouble?' Janet asked concernedly.

'We got word that Della's men might be ridin' in to wreck the two saloons yonder.'

'And you're going to try to stop them? Just the two of you?'

Mark thought he detected a note of alarm in her voice.

'There won't be many of 'em if they do show up. Della figures we're all back at the Circle X.'

'Be careful, Mark,' Janet said in a low whisper. 'You saved my father's life and I . . . we . . . wouldn't want anything to happen to you.'

'I'll be careful,' he promised.

'Whatever happens, you'll always be welcome with us.' There was something at the back of her eyes as she said it that Mark had never seen before. It made him think things that had been suppressed in his mind for a long time, for an eternity.

'Thanks. Once all this is finished, one way or the other, I'll take you up on that.'

She flashed him a warm smile as her father jerked on the reins and they drove off.

Mark watched until the buckboard had vanished along the trail out of sight, then walked back to Chet.

'Quite a pretty girl,' the older man commented. 'Reckon you could do worse than team up with her.' There was no jest in his tone. He was simply making a casual remark and Mark accepted it as such.

With the sun dipping down towards the distant hill there was still plenty of light in the street. The Golden Horseshoe appeared to have only a few customers inside and very little noise came out through the swing-doors. Even the tinny piano was silent.

Probably still too early for most of the Double T hands, Mark thought. But he had the feeling that if any of these gunslicks did ride in, they would get themselves fired up on liquor before they carried through Della's plan.

The two men remained standing on the boardwalk, watching the town, taking in everything around them. Mark rolled a cigarette, lit it and inhaled deeply. Beside him, Chet leaned nonchalantly against the post. Outwardly he seemed oblivious to what was happening, but beneath the brim of his hat his keen gaze flicked constantly in all directions.

'You think Driscoll was lyin' about Della's men hittin' the saloon?' Mark asked eventually.

'Could be.' Chet gave a terse nod, hitched up his gunbelt a little. 'If he was, and there is an attack on the ranch house, you can be sure of one thing. He'll be the first to get a bullet.'

'That's what makes me feel he was tellin' the truth. But so far, there ain't no sign of any Double T men in town.'

94

Chet gave a grunt as he straightened up.

'To my way o' thinking they won't try anythin' until after dark. The townsfolk have no likin' for Della although there's no doubt they're all real scared of her. But Clem has some friends in town.'

'Friends who might pitch in and help if they do hit the saloons?'

Chet grinned. 'If I were dead sure o' that, I might feel a mite easier in my mind.'

He turned and went into the saloon. A few moments later Mark followed him. There were five customers inside, all townsfolk. Mark ran his gaze over them, then walked to the bar.

There was the usual blue haze of tobacco smoke hanging over the tables inside the room. Here the air was a shade cooler and after the heat in the street outside it made a comfortable change.

'Not much doing tonight, Chet,' observed the bartender as he brought a bottle and two glasses. 'Ain't seen any o' the boys here at all today.'

'Most of 'em are back at the spread,' Stebbins replied. 'Della brought in more gunslicks today, brung 'em all the way from Kenton.'

'Hellfire,' breathed the other. 'You reckon she's gettin' set to make a move against the Circle X?'

'Clem reckons it's possible. If they do, we're ready for 'em.' Chet threw back the whiskey in a single gulp, poured a second and sipped this one more slowly.

Leaning forward with his elbows on the counter, the bartender seemed to have something on his mind. Then he straightened up, pulling a damp cloth from his apron. He began wiping up the liquor stains with it.

'You say none o' the other men will be comin' in tonight?'

'That's right.' Chet gave a nod.

Swallowing hard, the other remained silent for several seconds, then asked in a thick voice: 'Then why ain't you there if Della's goin' to make some move against the ranch?'

'Mebbe Boardman figures we'd be better off in town,' Chet answered shortly.

Mark noticed the expression which passed across the bartender's sweating features, knew that the other had drawn the obvious conclusion from his companion's remark.

'There's a chance she's goin' to hit this saloon. That's why you're here, ain't it?'

'Ain't nothin' for you to worry about,' Mark said quietly. 'I guess there's a back way outa here if you're figurin' on running.'

'And you reckon that'll save my hide?'

Chet pulled his Colt from its holster and laid it on the counter.

'Just carry on with your job and keep your mouth shut,' he said grimly, his lips scarcely moving. 'We don't want you shootin' your mouth off.'

For a moment the bartender's gaze flicked towards the scattergun he kept beneath the counter. Then he thought better of it as Chet placed his hand over the Colt, his finger inside the trigger guard. A moment later, the bartender sidled away and continued his wiping further along the bar.

Outside in the street, the darkness deepened with the sunset and lights came on, glowing yellowly in the dusk.

Slowly the minutes lengthened into an hour. Now it was completely dark outside. Mark had studied the faces of the men inside the saloon carefully in the mirror at the back of the bar. So far as he could tell, none of them were Della's men waiting to make their play.

Evidently, they were just ordinary townsfolk who preferred to drink in Boardman's saloon than in the Golden Horseshoe.

Beside him Chet fidgeted with his drink, his features tight. Clearly, the waiting was beginning to get to him.

Eventually Chet thrust himself upright.

'They ain't goin' to show up,' he muttered tersely. 'If Driscoll was tellin' the truth, they'd have been here by now.'

'Unless they're already in the Golden Horseshoe, stokin' themselves up.'

Chet shook his head decisively.

'Ain't heard anyone riding in for the last hour,' he replied sourly. 'Guess I'll give 'em another ten minutes and then head back.'

Mark shrugged. 'I'll take a look outside.'

'All right. But don't let yourself be seen. If that *hombre* Randers is with 'em, he'll recognize you on sight.'

'I'll be careful.' Mark moved to the door and stepped out on to the boardwalk. He slipped quickly to one side so that he was standing in deep shadow, away from the light flooding through the saloon doors and windows.

As far as he could make out, the street was empty. Nothing moved but a mangy dog on the far side, sidling along the boardwalk and then disappearing into a shadowed alley.

In spite of the quietness, a nagging little suspicion of impending trouble still gnawed at him. If Della had really fired Driscoll there was no reason for the man to lie.

Yet . . .

His head jerked up sharply at a sudden sound at the far end of the street. Narrowing his eyes, he picked out the four riders. They were walking their mounts slowly, side by side, not making the usual ruckus whenever they came into town.

Moving slowly so as not to attract their attention, he edged back into the saloon.

'Guess Driscoll was tellin' the truth,' he said in a low voice as Chet came towards him. 'Four men ridin' in. Could be Della's boys.'

Chet nodded. He pointed towards his left.

'You take one o' those windows. I'll take this side.'

Mark dropped to his knees behind the window and eased the Colts into the palms of his hands. From the corner of his eye he noticed the other customers pushing themselves to their feet, suddenly aware that something was about to happen.

'What the hell's goin' on?' called one of the men.

Mark waved him back with his gun. 'All of you get down unless you want your heads blown off. Della Rodriguez's men are on their way and they mean to shoot up the saloon.'

For a moment the men hesitated, still unsure of what was happening. Then, almost as one, they dropped to the floor, jerking out their guns. One of them, a whiskered oldster, wriggled forward until he was close beside Mark.

'You sure o' this, young fella?'

Mark could see that the others had had quite a lot to drink but they were not drunk.

'I'm sure.'

'Then I guess we're in this with you. I ain't got much liking for Boardman but Della Rodriguez is a she-devil.'

Risking a quick look, Mark saw that the riders had stopped just outside the Golden Horseshoe.

Keeping his voice low, Chet spoke.

'Hold your fire until I give the word. They ain't expectin' any trouble, possibly thinkin' they're just going to walk in and smash the place up.'

Outside, the men had slipped from the saddle. Now they were standing in a small group, talking among themselves. Then they spread out slightly along the boardwalk.

Mark studied them closely but saw no sign of Randers. That worried him. From what Driscoll had said, he felt sure Randers would be among them.

Across the street the men had ceased their conversation. They unholstered their guns and loosed off several shots, aiming at the windows. Instinctively, Mark pulled down his head as the glass shattered immediately above him. Flying fragments speared into the room.

Laughing loudly, the Double T riders advanced slowly out of the shadows The next moment, two of them dropped under the return fire from the saloon. The other two threw themselves back, rolling over towards the boardwalk.

As the stultifying echoes died away, Mark heard one of them yell to the other:

'Della said there'd be nobody here but townsfolk. How the hell did Boardman know?'

In the street one of the men who had gone down was struggling to lever himself up on one elbow. Raising his head to eye-level, Mark noticed the blood on his shirt just below the right shoulder.

Aiming swiftly, he sighted carefully. His slug took the other between the eyes. The man's head went back and he lay still.

More muzzle-fire leapt in blue-crimson flashes from the two men crouched in the shadows. Slugs cut through the smashed windows. There was the tinkle of broken glass as they shattered the bottles at the back of the bar.

Five feet away Chet and four men were firing rapidly. A sharp yell rose above the racketing din as a bullet found its mark. Gritting his teeth, Mark worked his way further along the wall. Through the broken pane he tried to make out the position of the fourth man. For a moment he saw no sign of him.

Then a slight movement caught his eye. Swiftly, he lined his Colt on the water-barrel where the other lay concealed. His finger was tight on the trigger as he waited for the other to make a move.

Before he could do anything there came a sudden shout from somewhere behind him. He rolled over swiftly and stared back towards the bar. At first, he could see nothing.

Then the bartender's head showed briefly above the counter. Alarm and fear were written all over his fleshy features. A moment later he scuttled out from behind the bar, one hand pointing behind him. Somehow he managed to get words out.

'There's a fire! Back yonder!'

Crouching down, Mark ran across the room.

'Keep that *hombre* out there occupied, Chet,' he called over his shoulder.

He bent and hauled the shaking bartender out of the way. Thick, oily smoke coiled along the rear of the bar. Swiftly, Mark ran towards the door at the far end and pushed it open.

An intense orange glow leapt at him from the far side of the small room. Behind it he made out two shadowy figures. Jerking up his Colt, he fired and saw one of the men stumble, clutching at his shoulder.

Then a voice called.

'We've done what we set out to do, let's get out of here.'

Mark recognized the voice at once. Ned Randers!

The bounty hunter caught at his companion's arm and hauled him away. There was the clatter of boots as Mark sent another couple of shots after them. With the smoke lacing agonizingly across his eyes, both shots missed. Inwardly he cursed himself for not considering this possibility earlier.

That frontal attack had been merely a feint on Randers's part to keep anyone inside occupied while he and his companion set the rear of the building on fire.

Choking as the smoke caught at the back of his throat, he yelled out.

'Some of you men fetch water or this whole place is goin' to go up in flames.'

His first instinctive reaction was to run through the flames and go after those two men. But he knew that

that would be useless. There would be a couple of mounts waiting not far away and he'd never catch up with them in the darkness.

At the moment the immediate need was to try to extinguish the fire. Already the flames had taken a firm hold on the wooden wall at the rear. He guessed Randers had brought oil with them to fuel the blaze, skirting around the edge of town while the others rode in openly.

Heat seared his hands and face as he grabbed at a length of canvas and began beating at the fire. Little rivulets of burning oil ran along the floor towards the door. Desperately, he stamped on them in an attempt to prevent them from reaching the inner wall.

If that should catch fire there would be little they could do to save the whole building. Ten seconds later three men rushed in with buckets of water which they threw on to the fire.

Swinging on them, Mark yelled: 'Douse this side o' the room. We can't save the outside wall but we might stop it spreadin' to the rest o' the building.'

The men nodded in sudden understanding, their sweating faces ruddy in the fiery glow. More water was brought from somewhere as the men struggled to keep the fire from spreading up towards the roof.

Then Chet was there and Mark guessed he had finished off the last man in the street.

'Hellfire. What a goddamn mess,' breathed Chet. For an instant, he stared helplessly at the blaze. Then, holstering his gun, he turned to help the men still bringing in water.

Thinning down his lips, Mark went to give a hand. The heat on his exposed flesh was intolerable. It was as if his bones were melting inside his scorched skin. From the corner of his eye he noticed the whiskered oldster beating at the fire with a long strip of heavy canvas, arms flailing like a demon.

Slowly they were succeeding. The rear wall was nothing more than a heap of smouldering ruin, grey-black ashes that were whirled away by the wind. But they had saved the rest of the building.

Leaning against the doorpost, Mark sobbed air into his heaving lungs. His eyes stung where smoke was still drifting from the piles of burnt-out rubble.

Beside him, Chet spoke hoarsely.

'Reckon Randers had this in mind all the time.'

'I should have guessed it when he wasn't with those others in the street,' Mark said, bitterly. 'I should have known he'd be around somewhere.'

'Did they get away?'

'I got one in the shoulder but Randers got away.'

'That critter's got more lives than a polecat,' grunted Chet.

Mark nodded but said nothing. He moved back into the saloon with Chet, where they waited until the rest of the men came from the rear, their faces grimed with the smoke. The bartender was still crouched in a corner, his arms over his face.

'Get on your feet,' Chet ordered roughly. 'Everything's fine now.' Bending, he caught the man by the arm, then hauled him upright. 'Now get back behind the bar.'

He turned to the five men.

'The drinks are on the house, boys,' he called. 'Thanks for your help.'

Several of the townsfolk had entered and were standing in a small knot by the doors. A moment later Whitman came pushing his way through.

'What happened here?' he demanded. 'There are four men lyin' in the street yonder.'

'Della's men,' Chet told him harshly. 'They were meant to draw everyone away from the back while Randers and another critter torched the saloon.'

'Goddamn.' Whitman walked behind the bar, glanced through the door at the end. Then he came back, his face grim. 'Could have been worse, I suppose. But Boardman ain't goin' to let this go. This damned feudin' has got to the point where the whole town ain't safe. It's got to stop now.' He looked directly at Mark as he spoke.

'That ain't going to be easy,' Mark replied soberly. 'Della is all set to stamp her authority on this entire town and territory. She ain't going to stop now.'

Whitman moved towards the door. Quite suddenly he seemed to have aged more than twenty years. Pausing, he glanced back at the two men.

'See if you can talk some sense into Boardman, get him to hold off. I'll ride out and have a word with Della.'

'Then I wish you luck, Sheriff,' Chet said. 'From what I know of her, she'll just as soon shoot you down as stop this feud.'

Whitman felt strangely helpless as he followed the trail to the Double T ranch. After what had happened at their earlier meeting, he knew he could expect short shrift from Della Rodriguez.

There were lights visible in the lower windows of the large ranch house as he rode up. A couple of horses were tethered to the rail which ran the whole length of the veranda. At the edge of his vision, he could just make out the long bunkhouse. Several men were gathered just outside.

He knocked on the door and waited. He knew Della had seen him ride up and had recognized him. The fact that she took several minutes before opening the door was clearly meant to show her disdain of him.

Unlike the last time he had seen her, she now wore a long crimson dress, her jet-black hair flowing in waves over her bare shoulders. In spite of himself he had to admit she was a strikingly beautiful woman, but this beauty was marred by the perpetual hardness in her eyes and the set of her lips.

'Sorry to bother you this time o' night, Miss Della,' he said apologetically. 'But there's somethin' I'd like to discuss with you.'

'Won't it wait until morning?' she asked coldly.

He hesitated for a moment, then summoned up courage.

'I figure we can thrash it out now, it might save a lot o' trouble later on,' he said.

'Trouble?' Her brows lifted slightly.

'Yes. Big trouble.'

'Very well. Come inside.' She stood to one side to allow him to enter. She closed the door and led the way into the parlour, motioning him to a seat. She sat down at the large table.

'Just what is this business you wish to discuss, Sheriff?' she asked tautly.

Whitman cleared his throat a trifle nervously.

'There was a little trouble in town tonight,' he said. 'Someone tried to torch one o' Clem Boardman's saloons. I—'

'I hope you didn't come here to accuse me or any of my men of that.' Her voice was as cold as ice.

'One o' the men who set fire to the back of the saloon was recognized. Ned Randers. Word is he's workin' for you now.'

Della rose lithely to her feet and stood glaring down at him, her dark eyes flashing angrily.

'Anyone who claims that Ned Randers was in town tonight is a liar.' She spat the words at him.

'Then you don't deny he is workin' for you?'

'No. Why should I? I choose the men who work for me. Some are gunmen but unfortunately it's necessary to have such men on my payroll with Clem Boardman continually threatening to rustle my cattle and run me out of the territory.'

'You got any proof that any of your beef has been rustled by Boardman?' Whitman tried to force casualness into his tone, knowing how quickly Della's fury could surge to the surface.

'I don't need any proof. When my steers go missing in the dead of night and Boardman's spread is right next to mine, there's no other place they can go.'

Whitman spread his hands.

'As the law in Ballards Crossing, I can't just go arrestin' a man on mere suspicion. But I figure you can see this feuding ain't goin' to get you anywhere. You'll just lose more men if you start a war with him.'

'This territory isn't big enough for the two of us.'

There was naked hostility in her voice now. 'I lost more than a dozen men at Devil Rock and that was Boardman's doing. But I don't see you harrassing him about it.'

'If you've got proof, solid proof, I'll bring him in. That's a promise. But until then, I want this in-fighting to stop.'

Della's full lips curled into a sardonic smile.

'Somehow, I don't think you're in a position to do anything, Sheriff.'

Whitman noted the emphasis she placed on the last word. He got to his feet. 'Perhaps the ordinary citizens of Ballards Crossing might have a say in that,' he said sharply. 'So long as you confined your fightin' to the ranches, well out o' town, that was your business. But when your feudin' affects the town, they might decide to do somethin' about it.'

For an instant, Della's eyes glared furiously. Then she uttered a harsh, derisive laugh.

'You reckon those fools dare stand against seasoned gunfighters. Why – I've only to give the word and my men will take your town apart at the seams.'

Tightening his lips at this rebuke, Whitman strode to the door. He knew that what she said was absolutely true. Even though the townsfolk outnumbered the men on her payroll by ten to one, they were not gunmen. He doubted if they would make a stand, even in defence of the town.

CHAPTER 7

RANGE FURY

The next morning, as soon as it was light, Mark walked out of the bunkhouse and into the courtyard. Louring dark clouds over the hills to the north-west promised rain.

Boardman had received the news of the events in town with mixed emotions. That four of Della's men had been killed in the street and another wounded, had obviously pleased him. The fire had caused less damage than might have been the case and rebuilding that part of the saloon was of little consequence.

The fact that Della had hit the saloon, however, had convinced him that she was now about to launch a full-scale attack on either the herd or the ranch house. To his way of thinking, it was evident she now considered herself sufficiently strong in manpower to risk such action.

As Mark rolled himself a smoke the ranch door opened and Boardman stepped out. Catching sight of

Mark, he stepped down and walked over. He had an expression on his face which Mark couldn't quite figure out.

Standing a couple of feet away, Boardman lit a cheroot and puffed on it for a few moments. Then he spoke gravely.

'You did a good job in town last night, Dalton, and I ain't goin' to forget it. When you rode in and asked for a job, I had you figured as bein' different from the men I usually hire.

'You ain't the normal type o' drifter who rides in askin' to be hired. The others are all gunslicks, men who reckon they're fast with a gun and determined to prove it but ride out over the hill if things get rough.' His features took on a speculative look. 'But I guess you got somethin' more on your mind.'

'Nothin' in particular,' Mark replied. He wasn't sure what Boardman was referring to, unless Chet had mentioned his meeting with Janet Casson.

Speaking through the cloud of blue smoke that wreathed his face, Boardman went on.

'You ride into town about the same time as this man Randers. I know you shot two of his companions in the saloon when they called you out. I also know all three of 'em claimed to be bounty hunters and you're wanted by the law for killin' two men in Colorado.'

'You goin' to hold that against me, Mr Boardman? I already know that Randers was the killer and the others framed me for the murders,' Mark said thinly. 'You've known all o' this since you hired me.'

Boardman stared down at the glowing tip of his cheroot.

'Sure – and it makes no difference to me whether you're outside the law or not. But my guess is that if you do get Randers, and finish what you have in mind, you intend to ride out.'

Mark pondered that for a few moments, not knowing what to say.

'That was my intention,' he muttered eventually. 'Whitman is a friend o' mine but there was no place I could hide out in Ballards Crossing while those three men were on my tail. When they threw in their lot with Della Rodriguez, I guess my position became even more desperate.'

'So you figured that if you came to work for me, it might give you a little time in which to sort things out.' Boardman tossed the butt of the cheroot at his feet and ground it out under his heel. He glanced up. 'If you kill this *hombre*, do you still intend to leave?' he asked.

Squaring up to him Mark replied bluntly:

'That was my intention at first.'

'But now you've changed your mind?'

Mark nodded. 'I guess that's right,' he affirmed.

'Mind tellin' me what your plans are?'

Mark shrugged.

'I guess there comes a time when a man reaches the end o' the trail instead o' riding from one place to another, never gettin' the chance to put down his roots,' he said.

'You got any special place in mind?'

'Maybe. I ain't right sure yet.'

Boardman made to say something more but at that moment there came the sound of a fast-running horse. A moment later the rider appeared at the end of the trail. One glance was enough to tell Mark that something was wrong.

The man was leaning forward in the saddle and as the horse swerved he fell limply sideways as if unable to hold himself upright. Almost without thinking, Mark ran forward, grabbed the bridle and hauled the animal to a sliding halt.

He caught the rider by the shoulders and lowered him gently to the ground. A wide patch of red showed on the rider's shirt at the right shoulder. There was a similar stain at the back and Mark knew the slug had passed right through without hitting bone.

He had clearly lost a lot of blood and could scarcely stand as Mark supported him. Boardman came running towards them.

'What the hell happened, Dan?' he snapped. 'Who did this?'

The other's lips moved, but for several seconds only a low moan came out. Then, with a conscious effort, he gasped:

'A couple o' Della's men jumped me. Guess they'd have finished me off only the horse bolted and I kept hangin' on.'

'I'll get the doc to have a look at you,' Boardman said as he and Mark helped the injured man to the bunkhouse. As Mark lowered him on to the bunk, the man spoke hoarsely.

'Somethin' you ought to know, boss. Della Rodriguez is gatherin' all her men. Reckon that's why those two bushwhackers tried to kill me.'

'You're sure o' this?' Tension showed clearly on the rancher's face.

The man forced a weak nod. 'I'm sure. She must've brought in another four gunhawks from somewhere. I figure there's close on forty men on the Double T spread right now.'

'Then it seems she's goin' to hit us real soon, probably tonight. I doubt if they'll try anythin' in daylight.'

'So we split our forces as you suggested earlier?' Mark asked.

'Reckon it's the only thing we can do.' Boardman scratched his ear. 'But with forty men to take care of, that ain't too hopeful.'

While one man was sent for the doctor, Boardman called all of the men together. His face was grim as he said sombrely:

'I reckon Della Rodriguez is goin' to hit us, probably after dark. And hit us hard. There'll be about forty men against us, all gunhawks. If any o' you men feel like ridin' out, now's the time to fork your broncs and leave.'

Staring about him, Mark saw to his surprise that not a single man moved. Boardman gave a brief nod of satisfaction.

'Good. Then we may have only a few hours to get ready for 'em. We don't know where she means to strike but it'll be either here or at the herd.'

'Could be that with all those men she'll hit both at once,' Hallam said, speaking for the first time.

'Then if she does, we'll have to divide our force,' Boardman said. 'I want half o' you men to ride out to the west pasture and keep a sharp watch on the cattle. The rest remain here.'

Half an hour later twelve of the men rode out. Mark watched them, them turned to Boardman.

'You want me to stay here?'

'I want you here, someone I can trust. I don't know what it is about you, Dalton, but like I said before, you ain't like the others. Before dark I want you to ride out with Slim and watch the trail from town. There could be a few of the townsfolk who'll throw in with Della now they know she's got all these men at her back. We might just hold off these men she's got but if another bunch takes us by surprise, we're finished.'

'Is that likely?'

'There may be quite a few and the two o' you won't be able to stop 'em all but you should be able to drop some of 'em before they get through.'

Shortly before noon the threatened rain started to pour from the heavens in torrential sheets. With it came an icy wind that bit deeply into their bones as the men went about the task of setting up defences around the bunkhouse and outbuildings.

The walls of the house and the large bunkhouse were thick and Mark guessed they would afford ample protection, but if Della threw all of her force against them, they could surround the entire place. If they came he doubted that they would risk a frontal attack across the courtyard.

From the windows fronting the wide area, the defenders inside could cut them down within seconds.

Through the blurring rain he scanned the area around the ranch house. There were two trails leading into the courtyard. Where the west trail began there was a stand of tall trees, their lower trunks choked with thick undergrowth.

This was by far the shorter trail from the Double T

and the one that, most likely, Della's men would take. If they had any sense they would make for that spot from where they could lay a screen of gunfire against the house without exposing themselves overmuch.

The wider trail which led into town was more open with little cover for at least 200 yards. That, he decided, would be the one any of Della's followers from Ballards Crossing would take.

Somehow, he doubted if there would be many in town who would side with her: only those who decided she couldn't lose and wanted to be in on the winning side.

That thought brought a fresh sense of frustration into his mind. His overriding aim was to get Ned Randers at the wrong end of a gun, wring a confession out of him, then hand him over to the law. So why had Boardman deliberately given him the job of watching the trail from town? It was almost as if the rancher didn't want him to come up against Randers.

He pushed the thought into the back of his mind, along with several others. At the moment, it was only necessary to concentrate on the job in hand.

By the end of the afternoon the rain had abated a little and the wind had settled down to a steady breeze. Boardman had spent most of his time going around the place, checking that everything was as prepared as it could be, that every man knew exactly what he had to do. At last he approached Mark.

He threw an appraising glance at the sky in the direction of the hills.

'My guess is that it's goin' to clear soon and there'll be a moon tonight,' he said. 'You two had better ride out and take up your position along the trail. If any do come that way, there shouldn't be more than half a dozen but I ain't takin' any chances.'

'Couldn't you send one o' the other men with Slim? This way, I won't get a chance at Randers if he comes in with the Double T riders.'

Boardman shook his head emphatically.

'I need Chet here and from what I've heard, you're by far the fastest man with a gun.' His tone brooked no argument. 'Now get – and watch yourself.'

Mark shrugged resignedly. There was no point in trying to get the rancher to change his mind. He took his mount from the corral, threw on the saddle and tightened the cinch under the horse's belly before climbing aboard.

Minutes later they hit the trail and set their mounts at a slow walk. The trail wound in and out of low rocky walls before they reached the pines.

Around them the silence now seemed charged with deadliness and menace. Once within the trees the trail narrowed and here Slim took the lead. In the past the darkness had given Mark a feeling of comfort but on this particular night it was different. A little warning itch started between his shoulder-blades and there was a crushing sensation of an invisible thunderhead hanging over him, like a storm ready to break.

A mile further on Slim reined up and pointed.

'There,' he said softly.

Peering into the darkness, Mark spotted a wide hollow to his right. It went back quite a way among the trees, a mass of midnight shadow.

'That looks as good a place as any to keep watch,'

Slim muttered. He turned his mount across the trail.

Mark edged the stallion into it, swung down from the saddle, led the horse back from the trail as far as possible, then stretched himself and settled down to wait with his companion.

It was possible, of course, that Della had sent word into town for more men but he doubted if many would follow her. Whatever they thought of her, few of the townsfolk considered this their fight.

They would wait to see what the outcome was and then side with the winner. It was the same old story, one which had happened in a dozen frontier towns. There was always this period of violence before a place could settle down and prosper.

Mark seated himself on the stump of a long-fallen tree and let his glance drift around him, still fighting with his frustration, wondering what was happening more than a mile away at the ranch. Slim built a smoke and stood with his shoulders against a tree.

The moon had just risen but as yet none of its light penetrated the overhead canopy of leaves and branches.

The minutes passed slowly and each one, as it succeeded the other, brought with it a heightening of the tension which lay like a coiled spring inside Mark. He realized that the waiting was setting his nerves on edge.

Every single muscle in his body was so tight that his limbs began to ache. Cramp threatened to clamp a tight hold on his legs but his mind was curiously clear and alert.

'There won't be anyone comin' from town,' Slim

observed after a long silence. 'Unless they come at the point of a gun.'

Mark pulled the collar of his jacket higher about his neck as the cold wind soughed through the trees.

'You figure Boardman knows somethin' we don't?'

At that moment the first racket of gunfire came. Mark instinctively jerked himself upright. Almost of their own volition, his hands dropped towards the guns at his waist.

Only with an effort did he stop them, letting his arms fall loosely by his sides. From the direction and intensity of the racketing gunfire he knew at once that the Circle X ranch house had come under attack and almost certainly by Della's entire force. The herd had been disregarded.

The first blasting roar of gunfire almost took Boardman by surprise. He had expected the attackers to ride up to the end of the trail and then advance on foot. Instead, they had clearly left their mounts much further away.

A bunch of them had settled among the trees at the far corner of the courtyard. Others were fleetingly visible some twenty yards away, darting from cover to cover.

Seconds after the first burst of gunfire from the Double T riders, it was returned by the men inside the bunkhouse. Crouching below one of the windows in the ranch house Stebbins had taken up a position beside Boardman. Eight other men were inside the house, watching at every window.

Outside, the moonlight was now sufficiently bright for them to see clearly to the far perimeter of the courtyard. Bright spurts of muzzle flame were visible as the attackers poured their fire against the building. But there was no sign of the men themselves.

Stebbins pulled down his head with a curse as the glass just above him shattered, fragments falling on to the floor all around him. Waiting for a moment, he slowly lifted his head. Squinting into the moonlight, he caught a fragmentary glimpse of two men running, doubled over, towards the wooden fence at one side.

One abruptly jerked as he loosed off two shots. The man struggled desperately to stay on his feet, to reach the comparative safety of the fence. He had almost made it when Boardman fired. The heavy slug took the man in the side. For a second, he pirouetted on his heels, then went down.

Carefully, Stebbins sighted on the fence, waiting for the second man to make a move. A slug hummed close to his head as the men among the trees sent a further fusillade of shots at the house.

With a conscious effort of will Chet held his ground, knowing the next bullet could have his name on it. Then the concealed man showed his head slightly around the edge of the fence.

In the same instant Chet squeezed the trigger, saw the head vanish. Then the other's body appeared as he slumped sideways into the dirt.

In a harsh, grating voice, Boardman called out. 'It looks as though they mean to rush us. Over to the left.'

Twisting his head slightly, Chet made out the knot of men close to the trees. Guns spitting muzzle-flame, they ran forward, spreading out slightly as they advanced.

From the adjoining room, a savage volley rang out. The rest of the men at the front of the house had also seen the danger. Four of the enemy dropped before they had covered ten yards.

The remainder faltered. Then, as if realizing the full extent of the firepower facing them, they turned and fled back.

Sucking air into his lungs, Stebbins thrust fresh shells into the empty chambers of his Colts, cursing softly as he realized his fingers were shaking. He snapped the chambers back into place and risked a quick glance through the smashed window.

Beyond the five bodies lying in the courtyard and the one near the fence, the others had almost reached the fringe of trees.

'Get those critters before they reach cover,' Boardman roared.

Stebbins tightened his lips, balanced the Colts on the windowledge, and squeezed the triggers rapidly, swinging the weapons slightly as he did so. A further two men jerked as the slugs hit them.

One man remained standing for several seconds, his arms reaching up as if clawing at the sky. Then he dropped like a sack of wheat, his legs sprawled in an unnatural position beneath him. Another continued to stagger for several yards before he went down. None of the men moved after hitting the ground.

For a full five minutes the roar of gunfire echoed around the house and adjoining buildings. Somewhere at the rear of the house a man screamed thinly. Then, strangely, everything fell silent.

Stebbins turned and rested his shoulders against the wall, breathing heavily. Dimly, he heard a man say: 'You reckon we've beaten 'em off?'

'Not a chance.' Boardman's tone was grim and decisive. 'That was just a try-out to test our defences. They're tryin' to wear us down. Next time they'll throw everythin' they've got at us.'

In the small hollow, Mark and Hallam heard the strange, nerve-tingling silence which followed the seemingly endless din of gunfire in the distance. Inwardly, Mark tried to figure out what it meant.

Either the men defending the ranch house had been overwhelmed by sheer weight of numbers or the Double T riders had withdrawn to consolidate. He was still fuming at his inability to do anything to help those men. But he knew Boardman had probably done the right thing in sending him here.

Some of Della's friends could be making their way from town at that very moment, hoping to be in at the kill. With their added support Boardman would almost certainly be finished. Those men who had been sent to guard the herd would very likely be out of range of gunshots and would know nothing of what was happening. Even if they decided to go against Boardman's orders and ride back they would be far too late.

As he paced the clearing with a restless unease he glanced down at the tip of the cigarette he had just lit. A riot of thoughts churned through his mind.

The moon vanished behind a bank of cloud. Its light vanished, and they were left in almost total darkness. The feeling of impotence was now so strong that he could scarcely control it. It was a constant pressure on his mind, something he could not rid himself of.

He tossed his cigarette away.

'I reckon we should ride back and check on what's happenin',' he snapped. 'We're just wastin' our time here.' He could see his chances of meeting up with Ned Randers diminishing rapidly.

A pause, then: 'I guess you're right.' Slim moved towards his mount, reached up for the bridle, then froze.

Carried on the wind, the faint sound reached them from some distance along the trail. Even though distorted by echoes, there was no mistaking it. A large group of riders were spurring their mounts in their direction.

'Seems like Clem was right,' Slim growled. 'Reckon there must be more than a dozen men in that bunch. Never figured Della had so many friends in town.'

'Better get ready.' Mark eased the Colts into the palms of his hands and crouched down beside one of the pines. 'At least we've got the advantage of surprise.'

Slim dropped down beside him.

'We're goin' to need more than that to stop this gang,' he muttered.

Carefully, Mark sighted his guns on the bend in the trail some forty yards away. All of his old instincts came back to him. Take down the first men and throw confusion into the others. At least, with the trail being so narrow, it would not be difficult to block it with bodies and startled horses.

He waited with a stolid patience for the men to show themselves around the bend. He disliked the idea of shooting down men from ambush without giving them a chance but in the circumstances it was the only thing to do.

At that moment the moon broke free of the clouds

and he was able to see more clearly than before.

The advancing riders seemed to be more cautious now, had slowed their mounts, evidently knowing they were approaching the Circle X spread. The first two riders appeared around the bend.

Narrowing his eyes, he sighted the Colts on them, his fingers tight against the triggers. Then he eased off the pressure.

The pale moonlight, glinting through the trees, shone on the star on the leading man's shirt.

'Hold your fire.' His voice was almost a shout. 'That's Sheriff Whitman!'

Beside him, he heard Slim's sharp intake of breath.

Whitman must have heard him for he lifted a hand, bringing the men behind him to a halt.

'That you, Mark?' Whitman called.

Mark lowered his guns and stepped out on to the trail. Cautiously, still suspicious, Hallam emerged and stood beside him.

The sheriff rode his mount right up to Mark. He glanced down with a faint grin on his grizzled features.

'We picked up one o' Della's men in town an hour ago,' he said. 'Eventually got him to talk, so we figured Boardman might need a little help.'

'Too damn right he does from what we've heard from back there,' Slim butted in before Mark could reply.

'We reckon that Della has sent all of her men to attack the Circle X ranch house,' Mark explained tersely. 'Boardman's outnumbered by at least two to one.'

'Then the sooner we get there and even things up

the better,' Whitman said. 'Maybe this is the chance I've been waitin' for to finish Della once and for all. I tried talkin' to her but she was having none of it.'

He waited while Mark and Hallam had saddled up, then went on: 'How do you figure we should go about this? Just ride in there and take 'em from the rear?'

Mark shook his head. 'By now, they'll have completely surrounded the place. How many men have you got, Hal?'

'Fourteen, not includin' me.'

'Then I guess that should be enough. We ride on for a while, then leave the horses. My guess is that most of 'em are under cover among the trees at the end o' the west trail. The rest will be all around the house.'

'Then we spread out and hit 'em from the rear where they'll be least expectin' it.' Whitman nodded his approval.

CHAPTER 8

COUNTER STROKE!

Ten minutes brought Mark and the men from town to the end of the trail. Ahead of them lay only darkness and shadows interspersed with patches of moonlight. They had dismounted 300 yards back, moving stealthily forward on foot.

Gunfire had erupted once again, coming from all directions but concentrated to their right. Now he was able to visualize how the Double T riders had positioned themselves.

Somewhere in that direction stood the tall mass of trees where he guessed most of the attackers were in place. It was an excellent vantage point for the enemy, covering as it did a complete frontal view of the ranch house and outbuildings. It also provided plenty of cover for Della's men.

Signalling with his hand, he motioned to six of the men to work their way to the right, around to the rear of the ranch house. Some of the enemy were there, their presence signalled by staccato bursts of sporadic gunfire breaking out at irregular intervals.

Leaning towards Whitman, he said softly:

'If we can take out those men among the trees yonder, I doubt if there'll be many left to continue the fight.'

The sheriff nodded to indicate his agreement and gestured to the rest of the men. Slowly and cautiously, making no sound, they moved off the trail and into the trees.

In the lead, Mark could just make out the tiny pinpricks of muzzle flame. He experienced a momentary creepy feeling as the gunfire rose sharply to an ear-splitting climax.

He could still see nothing of the men themselves, could mark their positions only vaguely from the gun flashes. There was also another thing that troubled him. He doubted if any of the men with him had ever fired a gun in anger. Whitman certainly had but he was a much older man now.

In front of them the firing died down momentarily and he guessed most of the men were reloading their weapons. Gently he worked his way forward among the trees, every sense alert. On either side of him the other men paused, then crouched down as he gave a signal.

The sound of rough voices drifted towards them out of the dimness and he suddenly realized that they were almost on top of them. Now there was no time to be lost. Levelling his Colts, he sent several rapid shots into the darkness.

A number of the slugs must have hit their targets, for the sudden yells that erupted were pain-filled screams and not the shouts of men taken by surprise. The next second the townsfolk joined in.

'There are some of 'em at our backs,' a harsh voice cried.

'How the hell did they get there?' rasped another.

Whitman sent a couple of shots in the direction of the voices. A moment later there was the unmistakable sound of a body falling, crashing into the dense undergrowth.

'Keep your heads down,' Mark yelled as the Double T men tried to turn to meet this new menace at their backs. A slug tore the bark from the tree beside Mark and he felt a sharp pain as it sliced across his cheek.

Swiftly he pulled his head down and crawled to one side as more lead slammed through the stunted bushes in front of him, humming over his head like a host of angry hornets. A short distance away one of the towners uttered a low groan and fell back with a slug in his shoulder.

More harsh yells rose as the gunslicks struggled to comprehend that the tables had been turned and they were now under attack from two quarters. Across the courtyard the men in the house were still giving a good account of themselves.

Two more of the men from town reeled back but the fire from the Double T riders was now diminishing rapidly. Then a small knot of men suddenly crashed through the bushes a few yards away.

Swiftly, Mark thrust himself on to one elbow, jerking his Colts around with an instinctive movement. Both weapons spoke at the same time. Two of the dark shapes swayed drunkenly, their guns falling from their hands. The third wheeled, firing at the same time.

A white-hot pain lanced along the side of Mark's right leg. Gritting his teeth, he deliberately ignored the agony as he squeezed the triggers again. The man uttered a harsh, bubbling cry and fell against a tree before sliding to the ground.

Completely encircled, the Double T men fought savagely, keeping their heads low, knowing that the instant they showed themselves they would be cut down.

Using what concealment he could, Mark crept forward a couple of yards. Now only desultory fire came from the men among the trees.

A moment later there came a harsh shout from a few yards away.

'All right. We're comin' out.'

Whitman's voice answered a moment later.

'Throw down your guns and move out on to the trail. Keep your hands raised. Any funny moves and we shoot.'

There was a pause, then the sound of men moving around. Mark got his feet under him and forced himself upright, grunting as pain lanced along his leg. Clinging to the nearest trunk, he waited for a moment until the agony subsided a little.

With an effort he forced himself to walk. There was the stickiness of blood on the side of his leg but, feeling it gingerly, he guessed that the slug had merely gouged a furrow along the flesh just above the knee without penetrating.

A few moments later he was back on the trail as the first of Della's men emerged with their hands lifted.

Whitman was there, his guns levelled on them.

'It sounds as though the rest of the bunch are nearly finished,' he said to Mark.

From where they stood, they saw that some of Boardman's men had come out of the bunkhouse and were now rounding up the few survivors. A couple of shots rang out and then there was silence.

Mark herded the captured men into the courtyard. 'We got these men, Mr Boardman,' he called harshly. 'Guess they're all finished.'

Ten seconds passed. Then the ranch-house door opened and Boardman came out with Stebbins close behind him. There was blood on the latter's sleeve.

Boardman walked across the courtyard, an expression of stunned surprise on his face as he saw the sheriff. His glance roamed over the townsfolk. Then his teeth showed in a faint grin.

'I figured Della might be sendin' more men from town. That's why I sent Dalton and Hallam to keep watch. I must say I never expected help like this.'

'Reckon Della made quite a lot of enemies in town,' Whitman replied. He glanced around him at the bodies sprawled around the house. 'But my guess is that she's finished now.'

'Any sign o' Randers among these men?' Mark asked tautly.

'If he ain't with this lot,' Boardman nodded towards the prisoners, 'then I guess he's dead.'

'Unless he's slipped through our fingers and got away.' Mark tried to conceal his frustration as he spoke.

*

Lying flat in the thick brush which clustered around the roots of the tall pines, Ned Randers had figured that Boardman and his crew would not have a chance against the gunfire pouring into the ranch just below. Inwardly he hoped that Dalton was among those men down there. He felt a sense of pleasure as he visualized the other lying inside when he and the others stormed the place.

The sudden and unexpected burst of gunfire from behind their position had sent a wave of panic through him. This was something none of them had anticipated. When Dalton's voice had come out of the darkness, followed by that of Sheriff Whitman, he immediately guessed what had happened.

Somehow, Dalton had not been with those men holed up in the ranch house. How he had managed to get Whitman and that other bunch from town was something he couldn't figure out. But now he was faced with the cold, hard fact that unless he did something quickly it was the end for him.

Out of the corner of his eye he saw the men with him get to their feet and toss their weapons away at the sheriff's ultimatum. Waiting until the last of them had drifted away into the darkness, he moved silently towards the northern fringe of the trees, slithering softly on his belly.

At any moment he expected to hear a shout and find a gun levelled on him. But nothing happened and a moment later he came out into the open where they had tethered their mounts. Here he waited tensely until he judged Dalton and the sheriff had taken the others down to the ranch.

Most of the men who had ridden out with him had been either killed or wounded and the latter would soon be in Boardman's hands. Della Rodriguez had played her hand – and lost. Somehow he doubted if she would be able to bring in more men to make a further attempt. Just like himself, she was finished.

What Whitman intended to do as far as she was concerned he didn't know. Sooner or later they would ride out to the Double T and he knew that Dalton would certainly be with them. The mere thought of Dalton brought a spark of intense anger into his mind.

The logical thing for him to do now was to ride out of the territory as quickly as possible, but he knew that Dalton would not let this go. Now that the other knew who had killed his friends, he would come after him.

As he swung up silently into the saddle, caution and sanity took over from raw emotion. First, he owed it to Della to inform her of what had happened. It was just possible that she still had important friends in town who would enable her to salvage something out of this defeat.

Quietly he walked his mount along the fringe of trees, every sense alert for anyone trailing him. After a little while he was able to convince himself that, for the moment, he was safe.

There was the chance that Boardman had sent some of his men to guard the herd. He had no wish to run into them. A mile further on he turned off the trail and rode into the hills towards the Double T ranch.

He was moving slowly along the bank of a narrow creek when he picked out the sound of riders in the distance. For a moment he considered giving his mount its head in spite of the uneven ground, then he pulled hard on the reins, bringing the horse to a halt.

The riders were some distance away but they were close enough to pick up the sound of a running horse. He drew back into the dark shadows and drew himself up in the saddle, scanning the terrain below him.

A few moments later he discerned the cloud of dust raised by several horses. The riders were moving swiftly, heading in the direction of the Circle X ranch. He guessed that these were the men sent to keep a watch on the herd.

He let the air go from his lungs and waited until they had faded into the distance before putting spurs to his mount's flanks. Sweat stood out coldly on his body as he realized he would have run straight into those men had he waited just a little while before making his break.

There were lights shining in the windows of the Double T ranch house as he rode up. Most of the way he had been running over in his mind how to tell Della what had occurred.

He stepped down and walked towards the door. The place seemed unnaturally quiet, almost as if it were totally deserted. Della stepped out on to the veranda as he approached.

'Well?' she asked sharply. 'Are the others rounding up Boardman's men?'

For a long moment Randers remained silent, the words he had been considering refusing to come.

Della stepped closer. Her face was expressionless but there was something in her eyes which ruffled the small hairs on the back of Randers's neck.

'Well?' she demanded again, her voice harsher than before.

'We were tricked.'

'What do you mean – tricked? Did you smash Boardman and his crew, or didn't you?'

'We had everythin' under control. The whole place was surrounded and only half of his men were there. The others were watchin' the herd and—'

'Damn you.' Her face turned ugly in the moonlight, twisted with fury. 'Answer me, will you! Why aren't Boardman and most of his crew dead by now?'

Speaking slowly through his clenched teeth, Randers said hoarsely: 'That *hombre* Dalton. He must've ridden into town because the next thing we knew there were a score o' townsfolk at our backs. We lost nearly all of our men before we knew what hit us.'

She ran her gaze over him, her features tight with a mixture of emotions. Randers had the impression that the full scale of the situation had not yet penetrated.

'Where's the sheriff now?'

Randers hesitated before replying. It was a question he had not anticipated.

'Back at the Circle X ranch, I expect.'

She turned. 'Come inside,' she said over her shoulder.

Unsure of what was about to happen Randers followed her inside. With a faint sense of surprise he noticed that she locked the door behind her.

'Stay here.' Without looking in his drection, she

walked across the room to the wide stairs. Slowly, she went up them and disappeared out of his sight at the top.

With a conscious effort, Randers fought down his apprehension. The feeling that something was wrong, not as it ought to be, pressed heavily on him. He had expected Della to scream and rage, to lash out at him.

It seemed incredible that she had accepted it so calmly. Whether she had considered this possibility and taken it into account, he didn't know. From her attitude it was almost as if she had another ace up her sleeve and the loss of all these men, her failure to smash Boardman, mattered little.

The minutes passed and there was still no sign of her. For a moment, he debated leaving. Then he realized there was no key in the door. She had clearly taken it with her.

His initial apprehension now turned into one of alarm. What the hell was happening here? Scarcely had the thought crossed his mind than Della reappeared at the top of the stairs. She had changed her attire. Now she wore the bright crimson dress he had seen once before. Open-mouthed, he stared as she slowly descended the stairs but she had almost reached the bottom before he noticed the whip she carried.

It was only then that he realized the full precariousness of his position. The feral glitter in her dark eyes held him transfixed like the stare of a snake. Then, his mind whirring, he suddenly dropped his hand towards the Colt at his waist.

Della's arm barely seemed to move. Rander's gun just managed to clear leather when the whip struck him. Coiling tightly around his wrist, his hand jerked up as Della tugged hard on the lash. The Colt flew from his fingers and slid across the floor near her feet.

'Della, what the hell. . . ?' he began.

The whip snaked out again and this time it slashed across his chest. Agony speared through his body as if he had been branded with a white-hot iron. Desperately, he tried to back away.

There was a noise in his ears which he could not identify, a crackling which was audible even above the pounding of the blood in his temples. Then, through strangely blurred vision, he noticed the smoke at the top of the stairs. It came rolling down in waves, thick and oily.

'You're insane.' He yelled the words at the top of his voice. With desperation born of sheer terror he flung himself forward. The whip came again, drawing a bloody weal down his cheek, just missing his eye.

Before Della could strike again, he swung his clenched fist against the side of her head. Her eyes blazing madly, she staggered to one side, but she did not go down.

Lips drawn back across her teeth, she hissed:

'You've all failed me. Everyone of you. But if Boardman thinks he's going to get his hands on this place, he's mistaken. Nobody will get it; I've seen to that.'

'You damned fool!' Randers forced himself to ignore the pain in his body. All he knew was that this woman intended to kill him and turn this ranch house into a blazing inferno.

Diving on to his knees, he struggled to reach the

Colt. A third lash of the whip seared across his shoulders. Then, somehow, his fingers closed around the butt of the gun. Squirming over on to his side, he swung up the Colt as Della loomed over him.

The gunshot was deafening in the room. He saw Della straighten. There was a look of stupefied amazement on her face as she stared down at the red stain, almost invisible against the dress. Then her features loosened.

A dribble of blood oozed from one corner of her mouth. A faint sigh escaped from her quivering lips as her knees bent and she fell to the floor in front of him.

For a moment he stared across at her inert body. Her eyes were still open, dark and mysterious, but there was no life in them. He drew himself up and stood there, swaying. The acrid smell of the smoke stung the back of his throat.

Coughing uncontrollably, he staggered towards the door. In his haste, he forgot that Della had locked it and he spent several precious seconds tugging futilely at it. At his back the rich drapes on the stairs were already blazing.

He knew it would not be long before the roof caved in, burying him completely. Without pausing to think coherently, he aimed the Colt at the lock, squeezing the trigger twice in rapid succession. Even though his hand was shaking violently, somehow both slugs found their mark.

He twisted the handle and pulled the door open with a thin screech of tortured metal. He staggered out into the cold night air, drawing it deeply into his burning lungs.

The roaring of the flames assaulted his ears, drowning out everything else. As he ran, swaying, towards his mount, he felt the heat scorching his back. He jerked the rope free of the rail and drew himself painfully into the saddle. Kicking spurs into the frenzied animal, he raced it madly across the courtyard, not stopping until he was several hundred feet away.

He turned and stared behind him. Flames leapt redly from all of the windows. Glass shattered at intervals with the effect of the intense heat. Red-glittering shards flew in all directions.

Shaking inwardly, he watched the scene through tear-blurred eyes, his mind a riot of thoughts. There was no doubt that this unexpected defeat had pushed Della's mind over the edge. But this was something he had never anticipated.

With a cavernous roar the entire roof fell in. Flames and sparks rose high into the air and drifted slowly away in the wind.

Even from where he sat the inferno's heat stung his face. This was something he had never bargained for, something which altered everything. The one person who could have afforded him full protection until he caught up with Dalton and rid himself of that menace for ever, now lay dead inside that holocaust.

He tried desperately to think clearly. Now he was more vulnerable than he had ever been. Very soon Dalton would discover that he was not among those men who had been wounded or killed at the Circle X ranch. Then Dalton would inevitably come looking for him – and with the sheriff and all of Boardman's men at his back. It would not be long before they found him.

The urge to ride out and put as much distance as possible between Ballards Crossing and himself was almost irresistible. It was not far to the Mexican border, but would he be safe even there? Somehow he doubted it. Now that Dalton knew he was the killer who had framed him, he would stop at nothing to hunt him down.

At last he reached a decision. From his conversations with Della in the past he knew there was one man in town who had been among her staunchest friends: Silas Carson, the lawyer. Whether he would help him was problematical but it was the only choice he had if he was to kill Dalton.

With twelve men at his back, Clem Boardman rode out to the Double T ranch shortly after dawn the next morning. Riding a little way behind the rancher, Mark sat easily in the saddle, his lips pressed into a hard line. A search among the bodies around the ranch house had soon revealed that Randers was not among them.

He felt certain that Randers would have accompanied those men; now he was forced to the inevitable conclusion that somehow the other had slipped away in the confusion.

'What do you intend doin' when we meet up with Della, Clem?' he asked tautly. 'You aim to let her leave the territory?'

Without turning his head, Boardman replied grimly.

'Depends on what happens when we get there. She may still have a few men with her. If she has, she might decide to fight to the finish.'

Mark lapsed into silence. That possibility had also

occurred to him. His impression of Della Rodriguez was that she would never surrender the ranch. Her hatred of Boardman seemed to transcend every other emotion in her, even to the point that she was prepared to die if she could take her enemy with her.

Half an hour later they climbed the low rise on the edge of the ranch. Boardman, slightly in the lead, abruptly reined up his mount. He was staring through wide-open eyes into the near distance, his mouth slackly open in stunned surprise.

Gigging his mount, Mark rode forward until he was beside him. Less than half a mile away the fire-blackened ruins of the once magnificent ranch house stood at the far side of the courtyard. Tendrils of black smoke were still drifting upward from where the fire was still smouldering deep inside.

'God Almighty!' Boardman breathed the words. He turned his head to look at Mark. 'You reckon she did this before pullin' out?'

Mark nodded slowly.

'Can't think of any other explanation. Guess she meant no one else to have the place once everythin' was lost.'

Around them the rest of the men were staring in stupefied amazement. At last Stebbins found his voice.

'You think we should ride down there and take a closer look, boss?'

After several moments Boardman pulled himself together and gave an affirmative nod. Slowly they paced their mounts down the slope and across the courtyard. An eerie silence hung over everything.

Boardman dismounted and walked forward with

Mark and Stebbins close on his heels. The stench of smoke almost choked them as they approached the shattered remnants of the porch. Clambering over the fallen beams, they made their way cautiously inside.

Piles of charred debris lay everywhere. The wide stairway had totally collapsed and now lay in a heap of smouldering fragments at the far side of the room.

Mark picked his way gingerly forward. He had gone only a few feet when he made out the arm protruding from beneath a mass of rubble. His sharp call brought Boardman running over.

Carefully, they eased the lengths of splintered wood aside.

'It's Della!' Incredulity edged the rancher's tone. 'She must've been trapped inside once the fire started.'

Mark stooped and turned the body over. The red dress now hung in tatters around her. Then he noticed the ugly wound.

'The fire didn't kill her,' he said hoarsely. 'She's been shot.'

'Shot? Then who. . . ?' Boardman knelt beside the body. There was a curious expression on his bluff features.

Stebbins sucked in a sharp breath.

'She sure didn't shoot herself. There's no gun here.'

'Randers.' Mark uttered the name like an oath. 'It had to be him. He torched your saloon and he'd not miss out on the chance to accompany those riders last night, if only to get at me.'

'You could well be right,' Boardman acknowledged. 'But there's no sign of him now. Whether it was him or Della who started the fire, we'll never know. But my guess is he's out o' the territory by now. Almost certainly over the border.'

Mark straightened up.

'Somehow, I doubt that,' he said. 'He knows that so long as I'm alive, he'll never be safe.'

CHAPTER 9

ACT OF TREACHERY

Darkness still lay like an ebony blanket over Ballards Crossing as Randers approached the town from the north. He had stayed well off the trails, even the narrow Indian tracks through the hills.

The chance that Dalton had guessed he had escaped and Boardman had sent men after him was small, but it was a risk he wasn't prepared to take. Too much was at stake now. The one overriding desire in his mind was to kill Dalton.

Had he and his companions succeeded in this when they had first trailed him to Ballards Crossing none of these subsequent events would have happened. He would now be somewhere else, enjoying the benefits of that bounty reward instead of running for his life like a hunted animal.

He had already made up his mind what he was going to tell the lawyer. Whatever happened, Carson must never know it was he who had shot Della, even though it had been in self-defence. Della and Carson had been close friends for many years. It was almost certain that the lawyer had been the driving force behind her acquisition of many of the smaller ranches when she had first arrived in the territory.

He guessed that few if any of these transactions had been legal. The owners had either been driven off their land or forced to sell at prices far below their true value. If Carson believed that Dalton had killed her, he would be less likely to help him.

Dust-stained and dirty, his face burned by that blazing inferno which had destroyed all of Della's dreams and ambitions, Randers dismounted on the northern edge of town. It still lacked a couple of hours to sunrise and he reckoned there would be very few of the citizens around at that hour.

In the darkness he edged along the narrow alley between two buildings until he reached the main street. Here he paused, checking everywhere for anything that moved. There was nothing. Not even a dog or cat disturbed the stillness.

Carson's place was in darkness, as he had expected. Not wanting to attract any unwelcome attention, he knocked softly on the door with the butt of his Colt. When nothing happened, he knocked again.

This time there came a sound from above his head. One of the windows opened.

'Who the hell is that?' came Carson's irritated voice.

Randers stepped back a little and glanced up. 'Ned Randers. One o' Della Rodriguez's men,' he said, in a soft whisper.

'Randers?' Carson hesitated, evidently turning the name over in his mind. Then he went on: 'What is it you want at this hour?'

'If you'll let me in, I'll tell you. This is important, real important.'

For a moment Randers thought the lawyer was going to tell him to go to hell. Then, without another word, Carson closed the window. A few moments later Randers heard the sound of footsteps on the other side of the door. A key rattled in the lock.

The door opened and Carson peered out at him, a lantern in his hand.

'All right, Randers. Come inside. And this had better be good, wakin' a man at this ungodly hour.'

Randers stepped inside and waited as the other locked and bolted the door. Then the lawyer went into one of the side rooms and motioned him to a chair at the long table.

'Did Della send you here?' asked Carson.

Randers sat down, shaking his head. He studied Carson closely in the lamplight. The lawyer was a tall, well-built man, darkly handsome, with a thin, clipped moustache.

'Della's dead,' Randers said, leaning his elbows on the table. 'I've just ridden from her place. Since you were her friend, I figured you should be the first to know.'

Carson jerked forward in his chair.

'Della . . . dead?'

On the table, his hand clenched into a tight first. Except for a tiny muscle twitching in his left cheek his face seemed as if carved from stone.

'And there's nothin' left o' the Double T ranch house,' Randers went on. 'Boardman and his boys burned it to the ground.'

The lawyer's lips compressed into a hard, thin line.

'Whatever kind o' man he was, I never figured he'd deliberately burn that place down with Della still inside.'

'That wasn't exactly how it was,' Randers said shortly. 'That *hombre*, Dalton, shot Della. It's a long story, but . . .' Randers paused and ran his tongue over dry lips. 'You ain't got a drink, have you?'

For a moment, the lawyer did not move. It was as if thoughts were distant things. Then he pushed his chair back, opened one of the drawers, and took out a bottle of whiskey and a glass.

He pushed them across the table and waited while Randers poured a stiff measure into the glass and swallowed it in a single gulp. He poured another, letting it stand in front of him, his fingers clenched around the glass.

'Della sent us all out tonight to hit Boardman and finish him for good. But that sheriff turned up with Dalton and a bunch o' men and they hit us from the rear. All o' the rest of us were either killed or wounded. I just managed to get away with Dalton on my tail.'

He took two leisurely sips of the liquor, then continued: 'I managed to throw him off along the trail. He must've passed me and ridden on to the Double T. When I got there the whole place was on fire. I heard the shot but by the time I reached the courtyard, he was spurrin' away and there was no chance o' catchin' him before he got back to Boardman's spread.'

'And you're sure it was Dalton?'

'Ain't no doubt about it. I knew him well enough back in Colorado and there was enough light from that fire to recognize him.'

Carson sat back in his chair, placing the tips of his fingers together. With an effort he had now regained some of his composure and now regarded Randers solemnly over the fleshy pyramid.

'If what you've just told me is true, then I guess the sheriff should be told. We've got this gunhawk on a charge of murder.'

Randers shook his head. That was the one thing he did not want.

'No! It'll do no good talkin' to the sheriff. He was dead against Della from the start. Boardman and his men will all swear Dalton was with 'em all night. I'd be just one man testifyin' against a couple o' dozen.'

'But—'

'Don't forget that with Della gone Boardman is now the big man in town. What he says goes. I've got some other plan in mind.'

Carson brought out a glass and poured himself a drink.

'If it means bringin' this man Dalton to justice I'm prepared to listen.'

'I need somewhere to stay out o' sight. Just for today. If I show myself around town I'll be tossed into jail.'

'So what do you intend to do?'

'I guess you know that small ranch some ways along the trail out o' town.'

'The Casson place. What of it?'

'When we were trailin' Dalton this way I reckon they

145

must've helped him. I think he stayed there for a little while before ridin' into town a few days ago. Just after we hit Boardman's saloon a couple of our boys said they'd seen Dalton havin' a mighty cosy conversation with Casson's daughter.'

Carson's brow furrowed.

'You meanin' to kill Sam Casson and his daughter? That would be a mighty stupid thing to do.'

'Nope. But if I was to take the girl, I reckon Dalton would come after us. Once I get him in a place o' my choosin', he's as good as dead.'

'And how will he know where you've gone?'

Randers grinned wolfishly.

'I'm relyin' on you to tell him. Once he rides into town lookin' for me he'll start askin' around. He ain't no fool. If you let it drop that I've gone out to Casson's place nothin' will stop him from goin' there.'

Carson scratched his chin.

'Could be that if he does go after you, he'll have a bunch o' Boardman's men at his back. Maybe even Whitman and some folk from town.'

Randers' lips parted in a vicious grin.

'That ain't Dalton's way. Like I said, I know him well enough to guess what kind of man he is. He'll come alone. He ain't goin' to allow any other man to get me.'

'You seem mighty sure o' that.'

'I am.'

Carson finished his drink and set the glass on the table.

'You'd better be. If you ain't, it's your life on the line.'

'And Janet Casson's,' Randers added ominously.

*

The Casson place looked empty as Randers approached it. There was a small herd of cattle in the meadow about half a mile away and the fencing looked stout and in good condition. Evidently, in spite of its small size, Sam Casson took pride in the place.

His mouth curled into a slight grin. So far things seemed to be working out as he had planned. Carson had put him up in the small room above the office and from there he had been able to keep a keen eye on everything going on in town.

The only thing that had puzzled him was that Dalton had not shown up at any time during the day. He had expected the other to come asking questions but there had been no sign of him, or any of Boardman's men.

Early in the afternoon, however, Whitman had arrived with a bunch of Della's men and locked them all up in the jailhouse. Apart from that there had been little going on which concerned him.

Certainly the news of what had happened to Della Rodriguez had spread like wildfire, and from Carson he had learned that a couple of men who had frequented the Golden Horseshoe saloon had abruptly saddled up and ridden out of town. Without Della to protect them, any who had openly supported her were suddenly vulnerable. Clearly those men were taking no chances.

Early on the morning of the second day he had ridden, unobserved, out of town, taking the wide trail to the south.

Now, just as the sun was rising, he dismounted near a small copse, looping the reins over an outjutting

147

branch. Stealthily he made his way to the rear of the small ranch house. He moved with caution, advancing from cover to cover. It was just possible that some of the hired hands were awake, going about their daily chores.

But he saw no one until he reached the corner of the building. Here, a sudden sound caused him to freeze in his tracks. There was the sound of a door opening and then heavy footsteps on the narrow veranda fronting the building.

He took out his Colt and thrust himself tightly against the wall as the footsteps approached.

A moment later Sam Casson came round the corner. Swiftly, Randers reversed the Colt and lunged forward. Some hidden instinct seemed to warn the other of his danger as Randers pushed himself from the wall.

Casson half swung, raising one arm to defend himself, his mouth open to utter a warning yell, but it never came out. The pistol butt crashed against the side of his head and he collapsed over the rail with a low moan, hanging there for a moment before falling on to the wooden planks.

Now there was no time to be lost. Quickly, Randers ran as silently as he could towards the open door. He had almost reached it when Janet Casson stepped out. For one startled moment she remained there. Then, swiftly, she ran back into the house.

Running forward, he reached the door. The girl was at the far wall, grabbing the shotgun from where it rested on a couple of pegs. Before she could turn, he levelled the Colt on her back.

'Drop it!' he rasped. 'If you don't, it'll be the last move you'll ever make. I ain't averse to shootin' a

148

woman in the back.'

For a moment Janet stood there. Then, slowly, she allowed the heavy weapon to fall on to the floor at her feet.

'That's better.' Randers stepped forward a couple of paces, the Colt rock-steady in his hand. 'You don't know how close you came to starin' death in the face.' As she turned, he grated: 'Now move away from that wall and you won't get hurt.'

With an expression of alarm on her face she stared straight at him. Realizing there had been no shot fired outside and her father might not be dead, she somehow of herself under tight control.

'What is it you want?' Her voice quavered slightly. 'We have nothing here worth taking.'

Her expression changed to one of startled recognition. 'I know who you are. You were with the other two men who rode here claiming to be bounty hunters looking for Mark Dalton.'

'That's right.' Randers waved the Colt menacingly.

She moved to the table, wher she stood regarding him closely, still afraid but determined not to show it. Her hands had a white-knuckled grip on the back of a chair.

'Dalton isn't here,' she said tautly. 'You can search the place if you wish.'

'No need for that.' Randers grinned. 'I know he isn't here. It ain't Dalton I want this time.'

Janet gave a sudden start and her grip on the chair tightened even further. Quite suddenly, she was really afraid of this man.

'Then what is it you want?'

'I aim to kill Dalton and you're goin' to help me do it.' Randers spoke harshly without taking his glance off her for a single instant.

'You're insane if you think I'll help you do that.' She tried desperately to force evenness into her tone. She knew that her position was extremely precarious, that this man would not hesitate to kill her unless she kept her head and did as he ordered.

'I reckon you've got no choice in the matter. You and me are goin' to take a little ride. When Dalton comes lookin' for you, and I know he will, I'll be ready for him. Now move!' His tone sharpened abruptly. 'Do as I say, or I'll put a bullet into your father. Right now, all he'll wake up with will be a sore head.'

'You'll never get away with this. Once Mark or the sheriff hears of it you're a dead man.'

'We'll see about that. By the time Whitman gets to hear of it I'll be long gone and across the border.' Randers turned and motioned her to the door. 'Somehow, I reckon only Dalton will come. You see, he wants to see me dead just as much as I want to kill him. His pride won't let him bring anyone else.'

He led her outside, towards the trees where his mount stood waiting.

'Where are you taking me?' Janet called loudly.

'The last place anyone will think o' lookin' for us. Back to the Double T ranch house.'

Keeping his attention fixed on the girl, ready for any wrong move she might have in mind, he took the lariat from the saddle and tied her hands in front of her.

'You get into the saddle,' he ordered briskly. 'And don't try anythin' or I'll put a bullet into you.'

Knowing that he meant every word he said, Janet caught hold of the pommel and somehow drew herself into the saddle. A moment later he had swung up behind her.

Had he turned to glance back towards the ranch house, he would have seen Sam Casson stirring slightly.

With the early sunlight beating down on his back and shoulders, Mark strode along the narrow boardwalk towards the Golden Horseshoe. For a whole day Boardman had kept all of the men at the Circle X. Mark had spent most of the time trying to get answers from the men they had captured, but with little success.

The only thing he was sure of was that Ned Randers was still alive, that somehow he had slipped through the net and vanished into the darkness. Now there was no doubt in his mind that Randers had killed Della Rodriguez.

He'd hoped that during the two days during which he had fumed and fretted at the ranch Whitman might have discovered something of Randers's whereabouts from the men he held in the jailhouse.

Yet the sheriff had learned nothing. Either those men knew nothing – or if they did, they weren't talking.

He pushed through the saloon doors and went up to the bar. This was the first time he had been inside this saloon. It was far larger than Boardman's and more lavishly furnished.

'A drink, mister?' The bartender eyed him strangely.

'Whiskey,' Mark replied. When the drink came, he said: 'I figured this place would be shut now that Della ain't around any more.'

The bartender leaned forward and spoke in a conspiratorial whisper.

'Carson is still keepin' it open. Him and Della were real good friends.'

'Carson?'

'He's the lawyer in town. Claims Della would've wanted it this way. Guess that's a matter of opinion but it suits me this way.'

Mark nodded, then stiffened as he realized that someone had approached him from behind and was now standing at his elbow. Turning, he saw the tall man who was eyeing him with a curious stare.

'I believe you've been askin' about someone named Randers,' said the other smoothly. 'I'm Silas Carson.'

Mark nodded. 'Seems he's just vanished after killin' Della Rodriguez.'

He noticed the sudden change of expression which passed over the other's features.

'You say he shot Della?'

'Couldn't have been anyone else. She'd been shot not long before we found her body in the ranch house. My guess is he's miles over the Mexico border by now, hopin' the law won't catch up with him.'

There was a pause, then Carson said thinly:

'This man Randers. Was he one o' those bounty hunters who rode in a little while back? Then he went to work for Della.'

Mark gave an affirmative nod.

'That's right. Why, have you seen him?'

The lawyer glanced around him as if afraid of being overheard.

'Saw him real early this mornin'. He was ridin' out of

152

town. Said he was headin' for some ranch along the south trail.'

Mark jerked away from the bar and caught the other by the sleeve.

'You're absolutely sure o' this?'

'Quite sure. Though what business he had there I couldn't say. I never had him figured as a friend o' Sam Casson.'

Hurriedly Mark finished his drink and left the saloon. Minutes later he was on the trail, heading south, pushing the stallion to its limit. All the way he kept his eyes open.

Carson had been a little too ready to tell him where Randers was and this could be a trap. If it wasn't, it was not too difficult to guess what Randers had in mind.

Randers meant to make him sweat, force his hand, hoping he would do something foolish. Mark guessed that, right now, the other would be holding Janet and her father at gunpoint, waiting for him to show.

By the time he came within sight of the ranch he had full control of himself. Only a grim anger rose within him now, making him cold inside, but his mind was perfectly clear.

No one was in sight as he reined up: the whole place seemed deserted. Then a figure appeared in the door-way. Sam Casson was holding a shotgun in his left hand while his right clutched at the nearby post as if for support.

Mark ran forward, instantly noticing the freshly dried blood on the side of the other's face.

'What happened here, Sam?' he asked urgently.

For a moment, Casson stared at him uncomprehendingly. Then he shook himself and lowered the weapon.

'He took my daughter, Mark. Hit me on the head and then made off with her.'

'You recognize him?'

'One of them bounty hunters who searched the place while you were helpin' me.'

'Ned Randers. I've been hopin' to catch up with that coyote since we finished Della.'

Casson's eyes clouded a little. Then he straightened and squared his shoulders.

'Della's finished?' There was a note of incredulity in his tone.

'She's dead. Far as we know Randers shot her. The whole place burned down a couple o' nights ago.'

'Then why should he—' Casson broke off sharply. A sudden gust of understanding spread over his features.

'You any idea where he's taken her?'

The old man forced a nod. 'I was just comin' round when he forced her yonder to where his mount was waitin'. I heard him say he was takin' her to the last place anyone would look. The Double T ranch.'

For a moment Mark's mind rejected that possibility. But the more he thought about it, the more logical it seemed. Like himself, Randers knew little of the territory around Ballards Crossing, knew nothing of any hideout in the hills. Furthermore, a man could conceal himself within those ruins and drop anyone approaching, particularly if he had a hostage.

He glanced at Casson.

'You'd better get someone to take a look at that wound, Sam,' he said sharply. 'I'll take care o' Randers.'

Casson's eyes changed and his lips thinned down over his teeth.

'I know you want Randers for what he's done to you, Mark. But Janet's my daughter. I'm ridin' out there with you.'

Mark opened his mouth to protest but one look at the expression on the other's face told him it would be useless to argue.

He waited impatiently while Casson hobbled across to the side of the house. When he returned he was sitting in the saddle with the shotgun somehow balanced in front of him. He looked like a man whose thoughts were somewhere in the distance and there was only one thing now uppermost in his mind.

'You sure you want to do this?' Mark asked, edging up alongside him. 'You're in no fit condition to face up to Randers.'

'Don't you worry none about me. I'll be fine.'

Shrugging, Mark turned his mount and touched spurs to its flanks.

They rode in silence for a while, cutting away from the town, Casson leading the way towards the hills.

'Ain't no sense ridin' into town and takin' the trail out from there,' he said laconically. 'That's what Randers will be expectin' you to do.'

'You know some way o' gettin' there without being seen?'

'Reckon I do.' Casson gave a wily grin. 'He can't watch every direction even if, as you say, that place is nothin' more than a burnt-out shell.'

They crossed a mass of scrubland which lay just beyond the border of Casson's spread, then cut up into the hills. Here there were few trails and those which they found were often steep upgrades where their mounts had to find footholds though there appeared to be none.

Mark glanced continuously at the man who rode just a few feet in front of him. He doubted if Casson had completely recovered from that blow on the head. At times, the old rancher swayed in the saddle, holding the reins in one hand and steadying the shotgun with the other.

Yet he gave no sign of faltering. Some deep, flaming anger inside him kept him going. Knowing how Casson felt, Mark hoped he wouldn't do anything foolish. Besides, he wanted Randers for himself, wanted the other to die and to know who had killed him.

It was almost an hour later when they reached the bottom of the pine-covered slopes. The ruins of the Double T ranch house lay about half a mile in front of them. To Mark it looked different from when he had last seen it only a little while earlier.

Then he suddenly realized that they had come upon it from the rear. In the harsh, glaring sunlight it looked grim and forbidding.

Casson halted his mount while they were still a couple of yards inside the trees. Weakly, he swung down from the saddle, held himself against his mount for a moment to regain his strength.

Mark climbed from the saddle and stood beside him as he pointed.

'There. See that gully? It goes all the way to the back of the place. Won't be easy but it's the only way to get there without bein' seen.'

One after the other, they scrambled down into the steep-sided gully. Here they were forced to crawl over the sharp-edged rocks which littered the bottom. By the time they were within twenty yards of the fire-blackened rear wall where great gaping holes had been burned through it, Mark's hands and knees had been abraded into raw flesh. Casson had fared even worse, having had to drag his injured leg behind him all the way.

Mark lifted his head cautiously and scanned the ruins. He could see no sign of Randers or the girl and guessed they were somewhere near the front of the building. That was where the gunhawk would expect him to appear.

'You stay here and give me time to work my way round to the front.' Casson whispered softly.

'Don't be a fool!' Mark hissed. 'The moment he spots you he'll shoot you down.'

The other shook his head determinedly.

'It ain't me he wants. He'll guess you're somewhere around and he'll want to find out where you are before he shoots me. Besides, he'll have Janet in front of him as a shield.'

Reluctantly, Mark was forced to accept the logic of Casson's remarks. Crouching down, he watched as Casson crawled away and disappeared from sight around the corner. He expected to hear a shot from inside the ruins but none came. Wherever Randers was, he hadn't spotted Casson.

Slowly he eased himself forward a little way. He hadn't liked the idea of the old man's going out there to face Randers. Casson was in no condition to face that killer, yet . . .

The harsh shout reached him a moment later from the front of the building. A moment fled before he recognized Randers's voice.

Almost without thinking he pushed himself to his feet and ran for the wall. Swiftly he thrust himself through one of the wide gaps.

All around him lay huge piles of debris, shattered fragments of glass, long wooden beams which criss-crossed each other. Trying to make no noise, he worked his way around them until he came up against the remnants of the stairs.

Randers was there, standing only ten feet away. He had one arm around the girl, forcing her to stand in front of him. Janet was struggling fiercely in his grasp but her hands were tied and her strength was no match for his.

'Let my daughter go, Randers.' Casson was standing several yards away, outside the ruins, his shotgun pointed firectly at the pair.

'Drop that shotgun, old man,' Randers snarled derisively. He lifted the Colt in his right hand and pointed it directly at the girl's head. 'If you don't, I'll put a bullet through her skull before you can pull that trigger.'

'Your fight ain't with her,' Casson shouted back. 'Or with me.'

'My fight's with anyone who gets in the way o' me killin' Dalton,' grated Randers. 'Reckon I should have put a slug into you when I had the chance.'

There was a brief pause, then Randers went on: 'Did Dalton send you? Reckon he's so yeller he didn't dare come and face me himself.'

Mark eased himself out into the open.

'Then reckon again, Randers,' he said quietly. 'I'm right here.'

For a split second, Randers hesitated. Then, with a savage movement, he thrust Janet away from him and whirled, swinging his Colt, hoping to catch Mark off guard as the girl uttered a harsh cry and fell on to the debris.

The two gunshots blended into each other, deafening in the stillness. Mark felt the fiery touch of the slug on his cheek. In front of him Randers swayed, staring at the widening red stain on his shirt. For a moment, he held life in his eyes, lips working but no sound coming out.

A gush of crimson came from between his slackly open lips as he fell sprawling across a charred beam.

Mark went forward, helping Janet to her feet as her father came hobbling towards them. She leaned against him, his arm around her waist.

'I knew you'd find me, wherever he took me,' she said softly.

'Thank your father for that. He heard Randers saying where he was takin' you and in spite of what happened to him, insisted on comin' with me.'

Sam gave him a knowing look which did not pass unnoticed by Janet.

'I guess you'll be havin' a talk with Boardman about leavin' him.'

Mark nodded, aware that the girl was watching him closely.

'I've a feelin' he'll raise no objection now that Della's no longer a menace. Boardman's ambitious but he ain't made in the same mould as her.'

Casson nodded. 'Once I've had a talk with Sheriff Whitman, I'm sure he'll let it be known that Randers was the man who killed your two partners. Then, with these bounty hunters all gone, you'll be a free man.'

Janet nodded.

'Free to go wherever you like,' she murmured softly.

Mark looked down at her.

'Sometimes that ain't the kind o' freedom a man wants after spendin' most of his time wanderin' from one place to another.'

From the expression on her face, and the warm glow at the back of her eyes, he knew she was aware of what he meant – and that it was what she had wanted to hear.